SAM

I'm still thinking about Miranda later on when in homeroom it hits me, or rather it falls right into my lap. Mr. Howe, who rarely does anything during homeroom besides grade papers and tell us to shut up, gets his fat butt out of his chair and says we need a new representative on the student council. This is perfect. Miranda Mullaly is the president of the student council. And how hard can it be to be a student council representative?

Duke

Then there's the spring musical. This year we're doing *The Pajama Game*. It's on the stage where I come alive. Auditions are next week and I simply can't wait. I haven't been this excited since, well, I suppose since the auditions for the fall show. I don't want to jinx it, but I'm sure I'll get the role of Sid and Miranda will get the role of Babe. It just has to happen.

CHOLLIE

Anyway, Mrs. Stempen drops all her papers on her desk and goes, "Okay, class, I have good news. We're going to start our semester projects today. I'm going to have you work with a partner for the project and lab by alphabetical order."

As Mrs. Stempen starts to call out our names, it hits me that my name is right after Miranda's and there's a good chance we'll be partners. And then it happens.

"Mullaly and Muller."

I like the sound of that.

Other Books You May Enjoy

ME & MIRANDA MULLALY

Jake Gerhardt

PUFFIN BOOKS

PUFFIN BOOKS
An imprint of Penguin Random House LLC
375 Hudson Street
New York, New York 10014

First published in the United States of America by Viking,
an imprint of Penguin Random House LLC, 2016
Published by Puffin Books, an imprint of Penguin Random House LLC, 2017

THE LIBRARY OF CONGRESS HAS CATOLOGED THE VIKING EDITION AS FOLLOWS:
Names: Gerhardt, Jake, 1970–
Title: Me and Miranda Mullaly / by Jake Gerhardt.
Description: New York : Viking Childrens Books, [2016] |
Summary: "The fates of three eighth grade boys converge in biology
class one day, as each falls desperately in love with the same girl"
— Provided by publisher.
Identifiers: LCCN 2015020368 | ISBN 9780451475404 (hardback)
Subjects: | CYAC: Love—Fiction. | Middle schools—Fiction. |
Schools—Fiction. | Humorous stories. | BISAC: JUVENILE FICTION /
Humorous Stories. | JUVENILE FICTION / Love & Romance. |
JUVENILE FICTION / School & Education.
Classification: LCC PZ7.1.G473 Me 2016 | DDC [Fic]—dc23

Puffin ISBN: 9780147516336

Printed in the United States of America
1 3 5 7 9 10 8 6 4 2

For my father,

Detective Jacob P. Gerhardt,

who taught us about love

and laughter

"I don't know what you think about being young. To me, it's a time for growing used to disappointment."

—John Mortimer

The Thumbtack

SAM

Until today, Miranda Mullaly isn't a girl I think about a lot. But she really gets my attention when she turns to me and hands me my thumbtack. I mean, she *really* gets my attention.

It all starts when I'm sitting in biology class, minding my own business and doing my best to mentally prepare for the long semester ahead. Even though it's only January 4, Christmas and New Year's seem like years ago. That's what school does to you. It kind of freezes time. It's only the first period of the first day, and already I feel like I've been stuck here forever.

As I'm sitting there, I'm thinking about the *new* me.

You see, I've finally decided to turn over a new leaf and put all my clowning around behind me. After all, I can't pull pranks my whole life. And my Christmas gift to my mom was a promise to clean up my act. If you think about it, this was a great gift because it made my mom very happy and didn't cost me a penny.

I mean, I'm so serious about all this I didn't make my usual stop to see the boys in the cafeteria. Imagine me, Sam Dolan, being the first person in class.

I have all this going through my head when Duke Samagura enters the room. He walks up to Mrs. Stempen, who is sitting at her desk with her head in a science book, and puts an apple in front of her. I mean, come on. Where does he think he is?

Duke stops and chitchats with Mrs. Stempen. God only knows what they're talking about, but I can take a pretty good guess. It's definitely about something boring. Duke's probably telling her about what he did over the break, like going to science museums and dissecting frogs on his kitchen table.

Everybody who knows me knows that by now I'm starting to get a little antsy. I'm ready for class to start and trying to keep myself from thinking about what I'm dying to do.

I can't help myself. I reach into my backpack and I take out a thumbtack. I hold it in my hand and even smile at it. My old friend, the thumbtack. We will part ways now that

I'm turning over a new leaf, and I'm going to miss it. That thumbtack and I have had a lot of fun together.

But when I hear Duke laughing with Mrs. Stempen like she's Tina Fey instead of a boring biology teacher, I can't help but think maybe this is one last hurrah for me and the thumbtack. After all, I can't be expected to go cold turkey.

Then I hear my mother's voice in my head. Like I said, she's really excited about my promise to be good at school. She even told me how proud she was of me before I left the house this morning. She's one of these moms who is really interested in education and all that stuff. So maybe it's best if I put the thumbtack back in my bag.

But I just can't. I mean, it's not against the law to have a little fun, and that's what the thumbtack is all about. And Duke is the perfect target. First of all, his name is Duke Vanderbilt Samagura. Add to that the fact that he dresses like a J.Crew model (What's with those guys and their pants that don't fit?) and he carries a briefcase instead of a backpack and, well, I'd be a fool if I didn't put a thumbtack on his chair. The way I see it, I really have little choice in the matter.

And since it's the first school day of the New Year, and January is a painfully long month, and Mrs. Stempen doesn't stop teaching from the moment class begins and is still talking when we're walking out the door—if you consider all that, I'm really doing everyone a favor. It's probably the only fun we'll have all month.

So I place the thumbtack on Duke's chair, pretty certain he'll thank me when he learns it's the last time I'll ever put a thumbtack on someone's chair.

And then the craziest thing that has ever happened in the history of Penn Valley Middle School happens. Just as Duke is about to sit on the thumbtack, *my* thumbtack, my *last* thumbtack, Miranda Mullaly puts out her hand and stops him.

This really throws me off. I mean, who does Miranda Mullaly think she is?

"I believe this is yours," she says, dropping the thumbtack into my hand.

She smiles at me, too. I don't know why I never noticed her smile before, because it's a good smile. I mean, it's a great smile. An excellent smile.

She smiles like she means it.

She smiles like she's happy.

She smiles like she *likes* me.

And she's got great teeth.

I take the thumbtack and put it in my bag and smile right back at Miranda.

Is this a great start to the New Year or what?

All I can say is wow! I mean, wow!

Duke

I'm man enough to admit it. I owe my parents, Neal and Cassandra, a sincere apology. They have been regaling me since birth with the story of how they first met. Allegedly it was love at first sight when they met and fell for each other as undergrads at Duke University, where they both studied sociology. They fell in love and have never been apart. I often gag when I hear them tell the story.

But as of today I believe in love at first sight. Today, I fell in love with Miranda Mullaly and she, if I'm not terribly mistaken, fell in love with me. How do I know? Because this morning, in biology class, Miranda stuck out her arm to keep me from sitting on a thumbtack maliciously placed on my seat by that rapscallion Sam Dolan.

And not only did Miranda save me from the embarrassment of sitting on the tack, she saved Sam Dolan's life as well. If I had sat on the tack, I probably would have smacked Sam Dolan's empty head with my textbook. And I would've been doing everyone a favor, since Sam Dolan fancies himself some sort of hilarious "class clown" and thinks it's his duty to entertain the school with moronic exploits, like a thumbtack on a *real* student's chair.

But I really don't care about the tack anymore. After

Miranda saved me, we gazed deeply into each other's eyes and something magical passed between us. "Her complexion was luminous, like that of apple-blossom through which the light falls . . ."[1]

She took my breath away.

Technically, this could not be considered love at first sight because Miranda and I have been classmates for years. But that is of little matter because I have never really *seen* Miranda before today. I now see her in a different light.

In order to better understand, I think the screenplay format would be helpful. And, since I'm probably going to write some movies after I've graduated from Harvard Medical School, a little screenwriting practice can't hurt.

Here it goes:

INT.—CLASSROOM—MORNING

DUKE VANDERBILT SAGAMURA, thirteen, handsome, enters the classroom. Duke walks to his desk and is about to take his seat when MIRANDA MULLALY, thirteen, stunning, puts out her arm to stop him.

1. This is how the poet William Butler Yeats described first seeing Maud Gonne, to whom he would propose marriage four times.

Miranda

I don't think you want to sit there.

(*Duke looks down and sees a thumbtack on his seat.*)

Duke

Thank you so very much.

(*Duke smiles at Miranda, then turns and glares at SAM DOLAN, thirteen, troglodyte.²*)

Miranda

It seems awfully immature, doesn't it?

(*Duke looks back at Miranda, appearing to really see her for the first time. Film slows, cue Handel's* Messiah, *their eyes sparkle.*)

Duke

One wonders when some people around here are going to grow up.

(*Miranda and Duke smile and gaze deeply into each other's eyes.*)

So there you have it. Or, as Damon Runyon³ would say, there, indeed, you have it.

....

2. Of Greek origin—a member of a prehistoric race of people that lived in caves, dens, or holes.

3. The great early twentieth-century writer whose stories were the basis of the Broadway musical *Guys and Dolls.*

CHOLLIE

Once I realize Duke Samagura isn't going to punch Sam Dolan in the nose, I get back to looking through my notebook for all those fancy vocabulary words Mr. Minkin is always making us learn. The reason I'm looking for all the fancy words is because my brother, Billy, is returning tonight and I need to tell him all about Miranda Mullaly.

Is this making sense? If it's not making sense, then this might help. I'm sitting in class and watching Miranda Mullaly, but I don't exactly know what to say to her. So I'm thinking I can get Billy's help, because Billy knows all there is to know about girls.

I really *noticed* Miranda for the first time at Christmas Day service. I was sitting quietly in the cold, dark church, trying to get comfortable on the wooden pew and trying not to look at the clock, when I heard a beautiful voice singing. It was really amazing. It was the kind of voice that reminds you of something happy and sad and hits you in the gut all at the same time. All I can remember about the song is that there was a drum and a boy. But the way Miranda sang it was pure magic. It suddenly seemed brighter, and I felt warm inside. Does this count as a Christmas miracle?

So anyway, I hear this voice in class and look up, and

there's Miranda Mullaly. She sticks out her arm and keeps Duke from sitting on a tack that Sam put on his chair. She probably saves Sam's life, because Duke can sometimes be a little crazy. And she saves the basketball season, because even though he messes around a lot in practice and Coach hates his guts, Sam's a pretty good point guard. And suddenly I can't think of anything but Miranda Mullaly. I'm not thinking about my new sneakers. I'm not thinking about what's for lunch. I'm not thinking about basketball practice. I'm not thinking about how long this class is. No, all I'm thinking about is Miranda Mullaly.

So, needless to say, I am *very* excited to be in science class with Miranda Mullaly, even though I'm sitting behind her and can't see her pretty face.

2

Battle Plans

CHOLLIE

I am very lucky Billy has been kicked out of college. I feel bad for him because my parents are pretty upset about the whole thing, but for me it really works out because Billy knows just about *everything* you need to know about women.

After dinner I knock on his bedroom door. Billy opens it and I take a quick look around. The room was just the way my mom likes it, and now Billy's made it into a huge mess. And it already smells. I ignore the dirty underwear and socks and find a place to sit, and we get right down to business. That's the way Billy operates.

"I got a situation," I tell Billy. To Billy, everything involving girls is a "situation."

"Okay," Billy says, finishing his push-ups and lying on his bed. "What's her name?"

"Miranda."

"I like it. I like it a lot. So what's the deal?"

"I really just noticed her at Christmas," I say.

"What made you notice her?" he asks.

"I guess hearing her sing. I really don't talk to her much. She's into books and getting good grades and that kind of stuff."

Billy sits up. "That's all right. Librarian types are okay in my book. Never underestimate nerds. Does she wear glasses?"

I have to think about it. "No, she doesn't wear glasses."

"That's okay. So now what's the situation?"

I tell Billy about the singing at Christmas and the thumbtack today and how she saved Duke Samagura from sitting on it and how I think that's a really cool thing to do.

Billy takes it all in. His eyes close and he concentrates.

"What else do you know about her?"

"Well, let's see, she's in the student council. She's always singing and dancing in the plays. She recycles all the time and complains about kids dying in other countries.

She likes to talk about the weather and says it's getting colder—or warmer—or something like that. I'm definitely going to start paying more attention to what she says."

"It sounds like you're hunting big game here, Chollie."

I nod and smile. Then he looks at me with a real serious look, the way a doctor on television talks to a patient.

"What you need is a battle plan. So here's what you want to do. Never throw out something that can be recycled. Learn a little bit about the Earth, whether it is getting colder or warmer or whatever. Lots of people are talking about that kind of stuff these days. You might even want to read a newspaper. Then you have something to chat her up about. Get it?"

"Yes. It makes total sense."

"Maybe find out which countries kids are dying in. Maybe do a school project about it. Are you following me? So let's say she's worrying about kids dying in Sri Lanka, you can do a project with her." Billy rubs his hands together. "Whatever you do, don't be one-dimensional."

It all makes sense to me. And it's all right in front of my eyes. I just need Billy to get me focused, kind of like needing a coach to get a team to gel. There's nothing better than having a big brother.

I get up to go, nodding. "Thanks, Billy."

"Oh, and here's another thing. There's probably going to be some stiff competition. Play it cool, Chollie. Play it cool. And watch out for these other snakes that are going to be smoothing on her. Strike while the iron is hot, and remember: the early bird gets the worm."

SAM

So there I am, walking down the hall with a big smile on my face and thinking about Miranda Mullaly. Out of the blue, Ralph Waldo comes up to me and starts blabbering on about something.

"What are you talking about?" I ask him.

"What did Sharon say?" he asks, practically drooling on himself.

"Oh, Ralph, you are a pain in the neck," I say, because that's what I really think. See, Ralph's in love with my sister Sharon, who's in the seventh grade. And since last semester Ralph has been giving me these messages to pass along, which are actually questionnaires. It's pathetic. And I don't give them to Sharon, because Sharon's my sister and Sharon's crazy. Just to give you an example, on Sharon's birthday she wanted to go to an art museum. I mean, an art museum? Really? And she reads these books by Jane Austen that are in English and sound like soap operas. You can tell Ralph Waldo doesn't have sisters simply because he thinks I talk to my sisters. I'm actually doing him a favor by throwing his embarrassing love notes in the trash.

"So, come on, Sam, did you talk to her?" Ralph really wants to know.

"Listen, Ralph, let me explain something to you about girls. . . ."

And then it hits me, right there in the hall by the main office.

It hits me that now, for the first time in my life, having two sisters might be an advantage. I can learn from them. I can observe them, the way scientists watch animals, to better understand them. Here I am, sandwiched between a sister in seventh grade and a sister in ninth grade. Of course, if my sisters had hearts and were normal, I could ask them a thing or two about the fairer sex, but, unfortunately, I have a special breed of sister.

So I take Ralph's stupid questionnaire and pretend to find a place for it in my back pocket but then toss it in the trash when I go to English class.

All I can think about all day is Miranda, and before I know it, school is over and basketball practice is over and here I am at home sitting at the dinner table. I didn't bring a notebook to record what they say, but I run up to my room as soon as it's over. Here's what I got:

Maureen (ninth grade): Is that my sweater?
Sharon (seventh grade): You said I could borrow it.
Maureen: I said you could *maybe* borrow it.
Sharon: I thought you said I could borrow it.

Maureen: I was going to wear it tomorrow.

Sharon: You can still wear it. It's clean.

Maureen: All I ask is people respect my things, is that so hard?

Dad: Please pass the peas.

Sharon: You can wear something of mine tomorrow.

Maureen: Your things are too small.

Sharon: What are you saying?

Maureen: I'm saying I can't fit in your clothes.

Dad: Please pass the peas, please.

I pass the peas to Dad and then everyone is quiet.

Maureen: Is your purple sweater clean?

Sharon: Yes.

Maureen: Maybe I can wear that tomorrow?

Sharon: Sure. You look great in that sweater.

Maureen: Do you think?

Sharon: Oh my gosh, yes!

Maureen: You look good in mine.

Dad: Is there any more chicken?

This is about all I can stand and all I can remember, but it's a pretty good start. Girls, obviously, like clothes and really think about what they're going to wear.

So here's my three-point plan:

1. Make a special point of noticing Miranda's clothes. Definitely compliment her on her amazing style, color scheme, etc.
2. No more pranks, no more thumbtacks. Miranda Mullaly is a serious girl and I'm really going to have to turn over that new leaf if we're going to be a couple. I even wrap up my favorite thumbtack in one of Mom's old scarves and put it in the top drawer of my bureau.

So my three-point plan isn't exactly three points, but it is a plan, and now that I have a plan, I feel pretty good about things. First thing I need to do tomorrow is make Miranda my lab partner. I'll ask her before class even begins, right after I say something nice about the clothes she's wearing. It's foolproof.

Duke

After school I further contemplated the Miranda affair. What I couldn't understand was why, exactly, she kept me from sitting on the tack? If I were a meathead like Chollie Muller, I'd probably go up to her and say something like, "Excuse me, duh, I was, um, wondering, duh, if you'd like to, duh, um, duh . . ." But I have a brain, and with a brain comes the ability to analyze situations. Unfortunately, however, I couldn't get the image of her smiling face out of my head. I simply couldn't think clearly. I didn't know what to do next.

I played with my dinner while both my parents, Neal and Cassandra Samagura, ignored me. They're sociologists and are pretty much paid to observe others, which is ironic, since they always ignore me. They're finishing up a book together, *Ethel's Story: The Untold Tale of Unplanned Pregnancy in Urban America*.[4] If I were a mean person, I'd introduce them to MTV so they could see their "untold" story has actually been told *ad nauseam*.[5]

....

4. The third book in their senseless series on the Voiceless in America.

5. Of Latin origin—to a disgusting or ridiculous degree; to the point of nausea.

Apparently Ethel's school, where Neal and Cassandra often observe her, is pretty crappy. God forbid they take an interest in me and see how substandard Penn Valley is.

Anyway, if they ever did get around to asking me how my day was, and that's a big *if*, this is what I would tell them.

It's not easy for someone like me to be a student at Penn Valley Middle School. The school is no good. The students are vapid creatures who think William Shakespeare is a rapper and believe Tupac is still alive. The teachers aren't any better, punching the clock, drinking from the public trough, and looking forward to their next undeserved day off. Mr. Minkin, my English teacher, thinks *A Separate Peace* is great literature.

Then I remembered Mrs. Stempen said we'd be choosing new lab partners tomorrow. I wished I could drop a note in Miranda's locker, but I don't know precisely where her locker is. So my best bet would be to strike up a conversation before class.

One thing was very clear: I would have to get Miranda's attention in an overt way. No more quietly getting straight As and leaving it at that. This was a woman with class, and, as Sherlock Holmes would say, this was a woman with a mind.

"How was your day at school, dear?" Cassandra asked me as we sipped our after-dinner tea.

I was about to comment on their poor parenting, but then a smile came across my face as I remembered Miranda's kind eyes.

"It was the best day ever," I told her. And part of me knew it was true.

3

Lab Partners

SAM

So there I am, walking down the hall, not bothering anybody, when Mr. Lichtensteiner comes up to me and gives me the third degree about the bathroom across from Mr. Blyweiss's room. I'm in a hurry to see if Miranda wants to be my lab partner, but Lichtensteiner is the kind of guy who thinks the most important thing in the world is for Penn Valley Middle School to run smoothly.

"You know anything about the boys' room across from Mr. Blyweiss's room?"

I'm sure somebody wrote something about Lichtensteiner on the wall and he thinks I did it. I get the blame for everything around here.

"Why don't you ask Mr. Blyweiss?" I say.

You would think Lichtensteiner would have enough sense to take my advice. Instead he does this whole tough-guy act, like he's one of these leg breakers from *The Godfather* or *Goodfellas* (two of my dad's favorite movies to watch with me on "date night").

"You know anything about toilet paper?" Mr. Lichtensteiner asks. Is this school weird or what?

"I know what it's used for," I tell him.

"Wise guy, eh?" he says, breathing his coffee breath on me.

I really don't have time for this. I mean, I've turned over a new leaf.

"I don't have time for this," I tell him. "And besides, I've turned over a new leaf."

Lichtensteiner nods his head up and down real slow, then takes a long look at me like he's never seen me before and he wants to remember my face. He smiles an evil smile and I can see the scrambled eggs he had for breakfast in his teeth and the hairs that grow like weeds out of his nose. It's all pretty disgusting.

Thanks to Lichtensteiner holding me up, I get to biology just as Mrs. Stempen is going on about the lab partners. Apparently last semester it didn't work out the way she wanted, and I have a feeling she's talking about me. You see, there was a little bit of a problem with some of the stuff we did in lab. And of course, everyone thinks it's my fault. But I only *suggested* taking the frog heart and putting it on a plate in the cafeteria. My best bud and lab partner, Jimmy Foxx, actually did it. I'm too grossed out by those things. And I still don't know what happened with the chemical reaction we got going that ended with fire alarms and an evacuation. Anyway, it's all behind me now, and since Lichtensteiner changed our schedules and split me and Foxxy up, I definitely won't be partnered with him again.

I'm really bummed I won't get a chance to ask Miranda to be my partner. I sit back and sigh because when you're having a day like this, there's nothing you can do but sit back and sigh. Mrs. Stempen calls Erica Dickerson's name and then my name. Erica Dickerson. Great. She's the kind of girl you see all the time and who always acts like your best friend. Oh, and she thinks she's really funny. But knock-knock jokes and the kind of obvious stuff anyone can find on the Internet are her idea of humor. Anyway, the *last* person I want to be partners with is Erica Dickerson.

But back to Miranda. I'm going to keep my eye on her, which is easy because she does everything around the school. She's a cheerleader. She edits the stupid school newspaper, which last year rejected my terrific idea for a feature called "Watch This! A History of Bad Ideas." The first installment would have been a behind-the-scenes story about the fire in the science lab. But the snobs at the school newspaper (not Miranda) don't have a sense of humor.

Also, Miranda always seems to be organizing things. She's the president of the student council, though I would never set foot in a room with those nerds who think they're better than everyone else. She's usually getting people to sign petitions for things, and she's especially upset about the goings-on in a whole bunch of countries that end in "stan." Obviously, I'll read up on the subject immediately.

From where I'm sitting, I can get a good look at Miranda. It's hard to describe what makes her so pretty. She's got brown hair that you just want to touch. And brown eyes that you just love to look into. And like I said, she's got terrific white teeth and an excellent posture. Watching her in class, you can see she has lots of energy and is very interested in what Mrs. Stempen is talking about. So she's kind of calm and energetic at the same time, which I think is pretty cool since I can barely stay in my seat for five minutes.

I'm still thinking about Miranda later on when in homeroom it hits me, or rather it falls right into my lap. Mr. Howe, who rarely does anything during homeroom besides grade papers and tell us to shut up, gets his fat butt out of his chair and says we need a new representative on the student council. This is perfect. Miranda Mullaly is the president of the student council. And how hard can it be to be a student council representative? Even Chollie Muller is a representative, so it can't be that difficult.

I throw my hand up right away.

"Yes, Mr. Dolan," Mr. Howe says, not even trying to care.

"I want to be on the student council."

"Okay."

Mr. Howe goes to sit back down when Erica Dickerson, my new lab partner, raises her hand. Mr. Howe starts grading papers again and doesn't see Erica's hand, which is fine by me because I think I know what Erica is up to. Erica begins to cough, then calls out, "Excuse me, Mr. Howe. Excuse me."

Mr. Howe looks up from his papers. "Yes, Miss Dickerson."

"I think we should have a vote."

"We don't need a vote, Miss Dickerson. Mr. Dolan is running unopposed."

"I would also like to represent the homeroom."

Mr. Howe huffs and puffs and sighs heavily. He is famous for looking at his watch throughout the day.

"Okay, raise your hand if you want to vote for Mr. Dolan."

I shoot up my hand and look around. No one votes for me.

"Okay," Mr. Howe continues, "who wants to vote for Miss Dickerson?"

Erica Dickerson raises her hand. It's the only hand in the air. Not only does no one else vote, but no one else even knows what's going on.

The bell rings and somehow all the jerks hear that. My homeroom gets up to leave. Erica Dickerson goes to Mr. Howe's desk. I follow her.

"Well, Mr. Howe, what are we going to do?" she asks.

"Why don't you let Dolan do it? He'll get kicked out in two weeks and then you can take over."

I'm about to give Mr. Howe a piece of mind, but I can't think of anything to say that would not get me in trouble right then and there.

"No, Mr. Howe. I think we need to have a proper vote," Erica insists.

"All right. Remind me next week and we'll have a little vote."

"We'll have to give speeches," says Erica Dickerson.

Mr. Howe looks at his watch again. Man, he must really hate kids.

"Okay, you can both have two minutes one day next week and then we'll vote. Will that work?"

I know he's delaying it because he figures I'll either forget about it or get in trouble. But not this time!

"Fine," Erica says, and walks out the door.

I follow her out of the classroom and think about saying something but decide against it. What a pain in the neck. Every time I come up with a good idea, somebody has to come along and ruin it.

CHOLLIE

This morning Mrs. Stempen walks into the science room all ready to go, just like Coach before a game. One thing I've got to say about Mrs. Stempen, she loves science. And I actually think she likes the students. Even Coach, who loves his players, sort of has a look in his eye at the end of the school day like he's super annoyed with kids and all his classes. And then, just like me, he comes alive again at basketball practice.

Anyway, Mrs. Stempen drops all her papers on her desk and goes, "Okay, class, I have good news. We're going to start our semester projects today. I'm going to have you work with a partner for the project and lab by alphabetical order."

I'm not the biggest fan of partnering up for anything. In the fall we did some kind of group project in history class. I didn't learn a thing because I didn't do a thing because Duke Samagura was my partner and he did all the work. So the research I did about Franklin Roosevelt was never used, even though it's really inspirational how he came back from being crippled by polio and all that. But for some reason, the teachers love to have us do group work.

As Mrs. Stempen starts to call out our names, it hits

me that my name is right after Miranda's and there's a good chance we'll be partners. And then it happens.

"Mullaly and Muller."

I like the sound of that.

Miranda Mullaly looks back at me and smiles and I smile back. Things are already going my way and I haven't even used Billy's advice yet.

But then Duke Samagura throws up his hand like it's on fire. He almost ruins everything when he says I shouldn't be partnered with Miranda since Kelly Muldowney is absent. Duke's like that, always wanting to help out the teacher. And I usually think it's pretty nice of Duke to want to always help out, but not this time.

Fortunately for me, Mrs. Stempen doesn't take Duke's advice. So now it's Mullaly and Muller working together in science class. I really like the sound of that!

I can't wait to tell Billy.

Duke

Thanks to Sam Dolan's antics in lab last semester, Mrs. Stempen has decided to assign our lab partners by alphabetical order. I knew something like this would happen. Sam was partnered with his friend Jimmy Foxx last semester. They just *had* to dissect the frog and keep its heart to throw on a lunch plate in the cafeteria. They just *had* to start a fire with pencils and pens and the Bunsen burner. They just *had* to mix volatile chemicals to try to create a reaction that set off smoke alarms all over the school. And you can bet the school administration got a letter from me.

First the thumbtack and now this. Was Sam's New Year's resolution to ruin my life?

And then, to make matters worse, Miranda was paired with Chollie Muller, superstar athlete who's about as sharp as a bowling ball. Not the worst guy in the world, though, especially compared to the likes of Jeff Gerson and Tom Kelly.[6] Still, one would think Mrs. Stempen would find another dimwit for Chollie and let me work with Miranda. I worked on a U.S. History project with him last semester

6. Bullies who think humor is stuffing a younger, more intelligent student into a locker and tossing his briefcase in the trash can.

and he was no help whatsoever. He thought the Great Depression was a mental disorder. Poor Miranda. She could be working with me.

After Mrs. Stempen announced the partners, I decided to lodge a protest.

"Yes, Duke?" Mrs. Stempen said, seeing my raised hand.

"Shouldn't Miranda be partnered with Kelly Muldowney?"

"Muller comes after Mullaly," Mrs. Stempen explained.

"Yes, of course, but aren't you forgetting about Kelly Muldowney? Kelly Muldowney should be partnered with Miranda Mullaly," I informed her.

From behind me some Neanderthal[7] whispered, "What's it matter to you, Samagura? What are you, in love with Chollie Muller?"

I chose not to look back and acknowledge my abuser and instead remained focused on the task at hand.

"Kelly can be partnered with Jeff Dugan, since they're both absent today."

"Oh, I see," I said very quietly and calmly. My mouth was dry and my heart raced and my blood boiled. And that's

....

7. After Neanderthal, a valley in Germany west of Düsseldorf, an extinct species or race of human beings. In Penn Valley a boorish, crude person; or just about half the male population.

when I decided to call in my friends Knuckles and Moose.

Knuckles and Moose wear suits with striped ties. Both have extremely flat noses and very hairy hands. When they make fists, they are like rocks. They are my good friends and keep me from getting in trouble.

Last semester there was an incident at school involving me, a U.S. History textbook, and Barney Dixon's skull. Barney called me a name (I honestly can't remember what it was now) and I countered by hitting Barney in the head with the textbook. The school nurse thought Barney was concussed (I protested that one needed a brain in order to suffer a concussion), and the school disciplinarian, Mr. Lichtensteiner, threatened to have me expelled. Neal and Cassandra promised to have me see a therapist, and within no time I was back in school, Barney Dixon was cured of bullying, and a therapist named Dr. Todd was happily ripping off my parents.

I must admit, however, that Dr. Todd did help by allowing me to summon up Knuckles and Moose whenever I feel like I may take matters into my own hands. In fact, Dr. Todd told me to imagine something different when I was feeling stressed or feeling as if I was going to smack somebody with a textbook. That's when Knuckles and Moose strolled into Dr. Todd's office and began to pummel him.

"Do you see it?" Dr. Todd asked, noticing the smile on my face.

"It works like a charm, Dr. Todd."

And Knuckles and Moose worked like a charm once again. I closed my eyes and imagined them straightening out my enemies in the back of the science classroom.

When it was all said and done, I was stuck with Nikki Shepherd, which is about as exciting as working with a dolt like Chollie. But I guess it could be worse. At least she's not drooling on herself like James Devine.[8]

But I can't get my mind off what could have been with Miranda as my lab partner. It would've paved the way to social engagements, future academic collaborations, and perhaps even marriage. Who knows? My uncaring parents, Cassandra and Neal, continued their academic work together at Vanderbilt after graduating from Duke.

---

8. You don't want to know about James Devine. Trust me.

4

Battle Plans—Part 2

CHOLLIE

All this week at lunchtime I meet up with Miranda Mullaly at the school library. It's crazy but I had no idea the library was open during lunch. What a great idea!

The library, if you haven't been there, has a lot of big windows that look out onto the garden and the football field. The garden's all dead now, but it'll probably look nice once it gets warmer.

Another cool thing about the library is that you can do whatever you want there. I don't mean like talk or play games, but you can grab a book and sit and read.

But anyway, the reason I'm even at the library is because Miranda Mullaly wants to start on our project. It really won't take us long, the way she gets right down to work. She types some stuff into her computer and scribbles a series of numbers and letters on a piece of scratch paper and runs off. Before I know what is happening, we have five books on the Brazilian tapir and the Amazon Rainforest. This is going to be a breeze.

Miranda tells me to find some information on their natural habitat, the food they eat, how long they live, how many babies they have, the usual kind of stuff you do when you have to do a science project. Miranda is going to get information on the rainforest.

She hands me two books, and I open them up and start looking through them but I'm hungry. I'm really hungry. I'm so hungry I can only think about the lunch in my bag. I have two peanut butter and jelly sandwiches, an apple and orange, chocolate chip cookies, and a thermos filled with tomato soup. So I can think about my lunch but not about what the Brazilian tapir eats. I look up at Miranda and she's already got like a page of notes and now she's drawing a map. Amazing.

Tapirs are vegetarians, so the book calls them herbivores. It makes me think of my lunch again, which is an herbivore lunch. A tapir would probably like to eat my lunch.

I don't know what to do. Do I tell Miranda I'm hungry? Should I offer her one of my sandwiches? But I don't even have to worry about it because my stomach rumbles, really loud, and, boy, is it embarrassing. I want to blame it on someone else but there's no one else around.

Miranda looks up at me and smiles.

"Are you hungry?"

"I'm so hungry it hurts."

"I'm sorry, I forgot about lunch. If you want to go have lunch and then come back, I'll be here until the end of the period."

"Aren't you going to have lunch?"

"I have to get started on this," she tells me. "Once the musical begins I will have little time for anything else."

I beat it out of there and I eat my lunch in record time.

When I finish telling him all this, Billy sits back up on his bed.

"It's not a bad start, Chollie. You really scored getting her as a lab partner. But it doesn't sound like you'll be able to smooth on her when she's doing her science work."

Billy's right.

"What's the deal with the play?" he asks.

"Oh, they have tryouts next week. Mr. Wexler, the guy who's in charge of it, was telling me about it today."

Billy lifts his eyes.

"You gotta get in the play, big boy. The play's the thing."

"Okay, Billy," I say. I'm ready to try out for the play

right now. I can't wait for science class and I can't wait for the play.

Then Billy gets a text.

"Okay, I gotta answer this. Good luck."

If I were a girl, I would give Billy a hug, I really would. Instead I say thanks.

Duke

I was in a rather rotten mood over dinner thanks to the lab partner debacle. Cassandra and Neal ignored me, busy reviewing notes and discussing their students at their second-rate college. I've been conditioned to accept their subpar parenting, so I wasn't particularly bothered. At least the chicken wasn't dry.

Alone in my room I reminisced about the three positive things that happened today.

The first was the toilet paper "decorations" in the boys' bathrooms. It was and is the perfect way to get back at Sam Dolan, the jerk. Today I decorated the bathroom next to the computer lab, then put Sam's math homework out on the windowsill. I'm sure Lichtensteiner is too dumb to think Sam's being set up. And since Sam stuffs everything in his pockets, his papers fall around him wherever he goes. It's a perfect way to get back at him for his attempted thumbtack escapade.

The second was the student council meeting. The student council, for the most part, tries to get things done, and at least there's a higher intellectual level. Maybe not on the student council *per se*,[9] since you get on the student council

---

9. Of Latin origin—of, in, or by itself or oneself; intrinsically.

by being voted in by your homeroom. I suppose Congress is much the same way; there are a lot of fools, clowns, and morons who garner votes fairly well and can do little else. But it's once the student council breaks into committees that the real work gets done.

And most importantly, the student council president is Miranda Mullaly, and yours truly is the vice president. I can't believe I've never noticed before how stunning she is. It was an absolute thrill to sit next to Miranda today and watch her in action.

Then there's number three, the spring musical. This year we're doing *The Pajama Game*. It's on the stage where I come alive. Auditions are next week and I simply can't wait. I haven't been this excited since, well, I suppose since the auditions for the fall show.

I don't want to jinx it, but I'm sure I'll get the role of Sid and Miranda will get the role of Babe. It just has to happen. And then will come the hours and hours of rehearsing and working together, dancing together, running our lines together. Oh, pure joy!

But before I get carried away, this might be as good a place as any to put in a little synopsis of the show. I do this not out of disrespect for you, dear reader, but simply as one who understands and has witnessed firsthand the inadequate education in this country.

The Pajama Game

Sid Sorokin (yours truly!) comes to town to run the Sleep-Tite Pajama Factory. His job is to get the factory running up to snuff and to keep the angry workers from going on strike. The leader of the union, Babe (Miranda—of course!) riles up the workers and challenges Sid's authority. Of course, in no time, both Sid and Babe have feelings for each other, but their romance is forbidden because they're on opposite sides of the conflict. Sid has to fire Babe, and their relationship is seemingly over. But then Sid learns, after an amazing dance number with Gladys (the secretary), that the boss is hiding money that was supposed to be a part of the workers' raises. Sid (me!) saves the day, and he and Babe dance a final number and live happily ever after.

Today during luncheon I met up with Mr. Wexler, the director of the musical. My original plan was to run lines from the show in the library, but Chollie Muller was there with Miranda. I was still a bit bitter about Chollie and Miranda working together. And then I saw that roisterer[10]

....
10. A rowdy, boisterous person; ruffian.

Sam Dolan in the library (he must've been lost), and I just couldn't take it. Fortunately, Mr. Wexler lets me stop by his room whenever I'm bored at school.

Personally, I think Mr. Wexler does an admirable job with the school musical, though some of my classmates would beg to differ. I'm not saying he's ready for the bright lights of Broadway, but I think he understands the level of talent at Penn Valley and works well with it. After all, if he casts yours truly for the lead, one can't help but agree Mr. Wexler knows what he's doing.

My only concern is Mr. Wexler's incessant obsession with having non-theatre people in the musical. I understand there is a dearth of males willing to go up on the stage, but opening up the auditions to jocks, troublemakers, and other intellectually inferior peers? Give me a break. Mr. Wexler has this idea it would broaden our appeal to the student population if we had a more diverse cast. I didn't want to argue with Mr. Wexler, especially before auditions, so I just nodded thoughtfully while Knuckles and Moose waited patiently in the wings.

Such are the sacrifices one must make in order to get ahead in the sordid world of the theatre.

SAM

We got Dad a whole bunch of old *Saturday Night Live* DVDs for Christmas. Since he mentioned it about a zillion times, it wasn't much of a surprise, but he's still really excited about it. I'm dying to watch *The Best of John Belushi* after dinner, but I have this student council speech to write. Dad is bummed when I tell him I won't be joining him for our movie. But a man's got to do what a man's got to do. So I dump my empty plate in the sink and I go right up to my room and get to work. If I want to get closer to Miranda, this is really important, especially since the lab partner thing didn't work out.

Just thinking about the lab partner thing gets me all worked up again. I can't believe Miranda got stuck with Chollie Muller. I mean, he's an okay guy and all, but watching them work together in the library, I can't help but think that she could've been working with me. She'd have such a better time. I'd have her laughing with some of the stories from "Watch This!" In fact, I think Miranda was in the school yard when Eric Dobson shouted, "Watch this!" and tried to shinny up the flagpole only to slide down right on his butt. Instead, I'm doing a dumb report on the dumb yak with dumb Erica Dickerson.

So, like I said, this homeroom representative speech

is really important. It's my only chance to get onto the student council.

But I can't even concentrate on the speech because I can hear Sharon singing really loudly down the hall.

I politely knock on her bedroom door. When she opens the door, I ask her and Maureen to keep it down. But she snaps at me and tells me that she's practicing for the school musical auditions. The play! The play that will star Miranda Mullaly! I forgot all about the stupid play. And even though weirdo Mr. Wexler, who runs the thing, mentions it to me almost every day, I still forgot. Where's my brain?

I try to find out more about this play thing.

"When are the tryouts?" I ask.

"Tryouts?" Sharon repeats. "They're not tryouts. These are auditions."

"When are the auditions?" I ask.

"Next Monday after school. And then there might be callbacks."

"What are callbacks?"

"Callbacks are when you get called back," she says.

It's like pulling teeth, talking to my sister. "And what do you do if you get called back?"

"You audition again." Maureen joins in. They both laugh at me and are really enjoying it. I ignore their immaturity and ask the big question.

"How do you try out, I mean, audition?" I ask.

"Don't tell me you're going to *try out* for the musical?" She laughs.

"I think I will. Mr. Wexler is always asking me to *audition* for it."

"That's only because there are never enough boys."

"Well, I'm going to anyway."

"You're going to have to sing a song," Sharon says.

"Any song?"

Sharon huffs and puffs at me the way Mr. Howe does in homeroom. I think she realizes it's rude to huff and puff and sigh like that, so she hands me a sheet of paper to make up for it.

"This is the song you have to sing."

I leave the room with the lyrics as my sisters continue to laugh.

Tonight I learn that girls, when they laugh, like to laugh together.

I can't figure out how I'm supposed to sing the song, and I give up on the speech. I join Dad and we watch the rest of the DVD. And even though it's super hilarious, I'm not in the mood. At least Dad is happy.

5

Freewriting

Miranda Mullaly

January 11, 2016

English 8A

Mr. Minkin

Suggested Writing Prompt: *If you could relive any day or moment in the last year, what would it be? What exactly would you change? How could that change affect you in the present?*

This is a difficult question because, of course, my mind is mostly on the future. High school, auditions for the spring musical, et cetera.

Still, the answer is simple. If I could relive any day from the last year, it would be the first day of this present semester. That morning, my mind was fully occupied with happy thoughts of my boyfriend, Tom Nelson. Oh, how I miss him. We had such a wonderful winter break together. We spent the days ice skating at the rink, sipping hot chocolate, and walking through the woods with the snow falling through the bare branches. It was magical. So I was probably smiling to myself, looking a bit like a fool immersed in my fond memories of Tom, when I thoughtlessly held out my hand and kept Duke from sitting on a tack placed on his chair by Sam Dolan.

Thinking back on it, I really don't know why I saved Duke anyway. I suppose it was simply because I'm tired of the childish antics of so many of my classmates. Tom would never do such a petty thing. Am I the only one who realizes that we'll be in high school in eight short months? Does anyone in my class even understand that you don't put thumbtacks on each other's seats in high school?

The way Duke smiled at me woke me from my daydreams of Tom and brought me back to Penn Valley. Duke absolutely beamed when I saved him. He can be so weird sometimes.

Because I couldn't bear to look at him for

another second, I turned around and gave Sam
Dolan the childish thumbtack. But looking at Sam
Dolan was no better. I can't look at Sam without
remembering the tooth he brought to school for
show-and-tell when we were in kindergarten. I
think it was his father's molar. I know that sounds
shallow, but he's just so gross. I dropped the
thumbtack in his hand, trying not to touch him.

So now it has been a week since I stopped
Duke from sitting on that lousy tack, and it's
almost like I saved his life instead of simply
saving him from embarrassment.

If I hadn't warned Duke about the thumbtack,
I would be able to audition for the musical
without him staring at me. And although I feel
very confident that I'll get the lead this year, I
really don't want the extra pressure.

If I hadn't warned Duke about the thumbtack,
I would have been able to sit at student council
without Duke blabbing on about the book his
parents are writing about a pregnant teenager.
Really? Have they ever heard of MTV?

(Is it too late to wish to go back in time twice?
I'd do anything not to have Chollie Muller as a lab
partner. Seriously, what kind of name is Chollie?

Who would voluntarily choose that over their given name of Charles?)

Now I'm starting to get depressed about not being able to go back in time. Oh well, time for happy thoughts, like when I see Tom again. Yay!

Sam Dolan

January 11th (right?)

English 8A

Mr. Minkin

Suggested Writing Prompt: *If you could relive any day or moment in the last year, what would it be? What exactly would you change? How could that change affect you in the present?*

Hey Mr. Minkin,

That's not a bad question at all. In fact, I like this question very much. It's almost like time travel, which seems like a pretty cool thing. I love time travel movies, and my dad and I have seen *Bill & Ted's Excellent Adventure* about a million times. We love that movie. Those two dudes crack us up. We love the part when the teacher says, "Who was Joan of Arc?" and Bill and Ted are like, "Noah's wife!"

But of course I can't go back *that* far. Maybe I would go back to the end of last year. If I could do that, I'd keep Foxxy from falling in love with Holly Culver. With Holly in the picture I've got no one to hang out with and things are getting kind of boring. Between him spending all his time with Holly, and Lichtensteiner splitting up our classes, it's almost like Foxxy has moved to another town and goes to another school.

Or better yet, I would go back to this morning. Then I wouldn't have allowed Erica Dickerson to go first for the student council speech. I also wouldn't have helped her out by holding up her visuals. But how was I supposed to know her posters would say, "Reasons Why We Should Not Vote for Sam Dolan"? Everybody thought it was real funny as Erica recapped the time our fourth grade class trip to the zoo was cut short because Foxxy and I had a little trouble with the monkeys. And then she retold the story from the fifth grade when I got stuck in a heating duct and the fire department had to be called. She had everyone in stitches recalling the time I accidently microwaved aluminum while on lunch duty when we were in the sixth grade.

With everyone laughing and having such a good time with Erica's speech there wasn't time for mine. But I told Mr. Howe that I changed my mind about being on the stupid student council anyway.

I don't want to represent a homeroom that thinks Erica Dickerson is funny.

But I'm not going to let it get me down, because this afternoon I'm going to get a part in the play.

Chollie Muller
January 11, 2015
English 8A
Mr. Minkin

Suggested Writing Prompt: *If you could relive
any day or moment in the last year, what would it
be? What exactly would you change? How could that
change affect you in the present?*

Dear Mr. Minkin,

Part of me wants to go back to Christmas
Day when I first heard Miranda Mullaly singing
in church. If I could go back to that day, I would
definitely stick around and look for Miranda so I
could talk with her. It's pretty hard to talk to her
in class because she's very serious about everything in school. But church is a different thing.
And if I knew I was going to go back in time, I'd
also have a whole thing written out beforehand
so I'd know what to talk about.

My brother Billy says it's very important to
ask girls questions to get them talking. Then you
pretend to listen to what they say. So I would
ask:

- What are your favorite church songs to sing?
- What are your favorite nonchurch songs?
- What did you get for Christmas?
- How is your vacation going?
- What are your favorite subjects in school?
- What's your favorite football team?
- What's your favorite food?
- Who is your favorite singer?
- What's your favorite movie?

Now that I think about it, maybe I should use these questions the next time we're in the library working on our science project or before the student council meeting begins.

Or maybe, if I could really go back in time, I would go back to the football game against Cedarbrook. I can still picture running into the end zone for the winning touchdown. If I could go back in time, then I would know that there was a defender coming at me from my left who was going to strip the ball from me, causing me to fumble at the goal line and lose the game.

God, it's killing me just thinking about that loss.

Thanks a lot for reminding me about it.

Duke Vanderbilt Samagura

11 January 2016

English 8A

Mr. Minkin

Suggested Writing Prompt: *If you could relive any day or moment in the last year, what would it be? What exactly would you change? How could that change affect you in the present?*

Sir:

   If I could go back in time, I would return to the first day of school. I would have taken one look at my schedule and walked into the office and demanded to have my English class changed. How is doing a writing prompt almost every day going to help us in English? Do you even read these? Do you notice that half the class does nothing when we have "Freewriting"? Are we getting credit for doodling? Can we meditate? Did you ever stop to consider that fifteen minutes of "Freewriting" is a waste of valuable teaching time? It's Monday morning and this is the best you can come up with for a lesson?

   Of course, if I really could go back in time, I

would go back one week, back to the first day
of the semester, to science class, then maybe
things would be very different. When Miranda
Mullaly looked into my eyes after pulling the
thumbtack from my chair, I would have taken her
by the hand and led her from the room. I would
have taken her away from this school filled with
ignoramuses and dolts. We would've gone for
a walk in the park, where we could simply be
together, away from our indolent classmates.

6

Tryouts & Auditions

SAM

I can't understand this obsession Lichtensteiner has with toilet paper, but it's starting to get on my nerves. Again, here I am strolling the hallway on my way to class, the epitome of a model student who is turning over a new leaf, and Lichtensteiner comes out of nowhere and stops me and starts talking about toilet paper. I'm starting to get sick of it.

Anyway, I rush off to the auditorium for these tryouts or auditions or whatever they're called. Mr. Wexler, who's a little bit too excited about the whole thing, if you ask me, tells me and Chollie we can audition first and then head off to basketball practice. Why Chollie wants to be in the play is beyond me, but who cares.

So anyway, here I am up on the stage. Of course, I

don't really know what they expect me to do. I'm thinking maybe it won't be that bad. It can't be worse than the student council speeches. But since I lost my chance to be on student council with Miranda Mullaly, I really have to get into this play, even though, like I said, it's not my thing. I mean, who really wants to be in the play with nerds like Duke and Ralph and my sister? But when I see Miranda sitting out there in the audience, I figure I can hold my nose and go for it.

Even though people don't think I get nervous, since I fool around in class sometimes, my knees are shaking. I'm nervous and I know I look nervous, too. And unlike Duke Samagura, who probably dreams all the time about dancing and singing, I haven't been in anything since elementary school, which is when they make *everyone* go up onstage. And you don't have to try out in elementary school. So, to tell the truth, I'm fairly nervous.

Sharon is no help, either. She gave me the lyrics but she didn't help with the melody or tune or whatever it is. And of course I'm not going to spend my night singing with my sister. She did say to "wow them," but even that doesn't make much sense to me.

But it all doesn't matter because there I am, up onstage, and everyone's waiting for me to sing. Mr. Wexler, who's wearing this weird red hat, and Miss Kerrigan, an

English teacher who's a real nut about English class and big words, are sitting out there with legal pads, serious as can be.

I channel my inner Andy Samberg and rap out "Hey There" to the tune of "Lazy Sunday." It's harder than it looks, but I think I do a pretty good job, rapping like I've been rapping my whole life and trying my best to "wow them."

By the time I'm done, I'm sort of out of it. Sometimes, when I'm really nervous, things kind of slow down and my vision gets blurry. Weird, right? So as I'm rapping I can't see too far in front of me, which is a good thing because I really don't want to do it in front of the whole school anyway.

Slowly, everything starts working again. My vision gets clear and sounds become sharper and the world goes back to regular speed. And what do I see? Mr. Wexler, the old bugger, has a big smile on his face and he's clapping. So is Miss Kerrigan. She's clapping along with him.

So all in all, I guess it went pretty well.

But just in case, I jump off the stage and rush off to basketball practice, keeping my eye out for that lunatic Lichtensteiner.

What a day.

Duke

I skipped out a little early from art class to toss some toilet paper on the walls of the second-floor bathroom. No one saw me, and the world's worst art teacher, Mr. O'Reiley (a huge joke who thinks the garbage my classmates create should hang in the Louvre[11]), never even noticed I left class.

I was the first to get to the auditorium, but good old Mr. Wexler, who'd donned a red beret (a nice touch, I thought), was already there, sitting in the middle row alongside Miss Kerrigan.

With great excitement and enthusiasm, I took a seat to their right. But I waited and I waited and I wasn't sure what was going on. Being a man of action, I approached the two so they would know I was not playing games. You really don't want to go into an audition not ready to go. And I was ready to go.

"Good afternoon, Mr. Wexler. I'm ready when you are."

"Great, Duke, super. Just take a seat and we'll call you."

This was not the reaction I was expecting. Still, Mr. Wexler was in charge, so I took my seat. More and more

11. Perhaps the world's greatest museum, located in Paris, France. Mr. O'Reiley's unflinchingly positive feedback is a perfect example of the disaster "self-esteem" has wrought on American education.

students trickled in. After a few minutes it was obvious Mr. Wexler was waiting for someone.

"What are we waiting for, Mr. Wexler?" I asked.

"I told some of the basketball players they could audition before practice began. Oh, here they are now." Mr. Wexler smiled as Chollie Muller and Sam Dolan walked down the aisle. It was disgusting.

Mr. Wexler turned to Miss Kerrigan. "Isn't this fantastic?"

If I were a vengeful person I would return to Penn Valley in five years and put sugar in Mr. Wexler's gas tank. What a moron. No, Mr. Wexler, it isn't fantastic. Theatre is not something one just throws oneself into for a lark or on a whim. It's a passion. It's a way of life.

I had no choice but to sit and watch these two massacre the great lyrics and melodies from a timeless work of art. For a person with a brain and respect for theatre, it was torture, pure torture.

At first I was so angry my hands were shaking. But once I saw Chollie Muller try to audition, I laughed it off.

"From the top," Mr. Wexler said, handing him the lyrics.

Chollie just stood there with the stupid "Huh?" expression he wears every second of the day.

"From the top," Mr. Wexler repeated, a little too kindly, in my opinion. This was an audition, for heaven's sake.

"The top of what?" Chollie managed to ask.

It took every ounce of self-control to not yell out, "Fraud! Fraud! He doesn't love musical theatre. He doesn't even know what it is. He has no respect for the art or the artist. Get that bum off the stage!"

Somehow I kept control. It helps to have class. And Knuckles and Moose.

"We need to hear your voice. Can you sing that song?" Mr. Wexler asked.

"I don't know how it goes."

"Can you sing something?" Mr. Wexler asked, leading him along.

Chollie shrugged. You would've thought Mr. Wexler had asked him a question about nuclear physics.

"How about 'Mary Had a Little Lamb'?" Mr. Wexler asked.

Like a three-year-old, Chollie nodded. Mr. Wexler pointed to Mrs. Lambert, and she accompanied Chollie as he sang "Mary Had a Little Lamb."

Everyone thought it was great fun. I couldn't believe it. Even Ralph Waldo, my chief rival for the role of Sid, yelled, "Encore!" and meant it! And when I looked back, Miranda had a smile on her face. Incredible.

Mercifully, Chollie was done. Next up was Sam Dolan.

Unlike Chollie, Sam was ready to go. "I'm going to perform 'Hey There,'" he told Mr. Wexler, as if he'd been auditioning his entire life.

Mrs. Lambert started to play the accompaniment on the piano.

"Oh, I won't need the piano," Sam said.

Mr. Wexler raised his eyebrows as if he was very impressed. I was about to be sick.

Then Sam snapped his fingers and started rapping the lyrics to "Hey There" as if he were one of Cassandra and Neal's subjects.[12]

I was shocked, utterly shocked. This is how civilizations crumble.

Personally, I thought Sam Dolan should have been tossed from the auditorium, and I smiled to myself imagining Knuckles and Moose dragging him off the stage. But my revelry ended when I saw Mr. Wexler applauding, eating it up like a pig at a trough.

"Well done, Sam! Well done, indeed. Very interesting interpretation," Mr. Wexler gushed.

Sam left and the travesty was over. And I left as well, needing a moment to collect my thoughts, breathe deeply,

....

12. Their third book, *Christ, the King of Rap*, was about the Christian roots of hip-hop. Not their best effort.

count to ten, and shake the disgraceful auditions from my mind.

After pacing the halls and mentally preparing for my audition, I walked back to the auditorium to the sound of the mellifluous voice of Miranda belting out "I'm Not at All in Love." A smile broke over my face, my anger receded. At last, true talent! I was ready once again for the audition of a lifetime.

It was quite a shock, however, to see that the heavenly singing came from Sharon Dolan, Sam's younger sister. She finished and the crowd cheered as I searched for Miranda. But she was gone.

No matter, for we would be onstage together soon enough.

I was called up next. And I proved I am not made of sugar candy,[13] nailing my audition with a crowd-pleasing rendition of "Once a Year Day."

Yours truly, in my opinion, single-handedly restored some sanity to the asylum otherwise known as Penn Valley Middle School.

....

13. Paraphrasing Winston Churchill. The full quote is: "We have not journeyed across the centuries, across the oceans, across the mountains, across the prairies, because we are made of sugar candy."

CHOLLIE

Boy, do I feel really good about everything.

Trying out for the play isn't easy. I'm really sweating up there onstage with everybody watching. And it's weird sweating when you're not running around. I sort of feel like I'm in trouble, but all I really have to do is sing a song. There are tons of people watching and waiting for their turn to try out, but it's all okay when I see Miranda Mullaly in the back. And what's so hard about singing "Mary Had a Little Lamb"? Mr. Wexler even has someone playing the piano for me. If you haven't ever sung a song like that out of the blue, a little background music helps a lot.

Billy says it's because I'm in love, and he teases me a bit when I tell him. But I don't care at all because I feel so good.

Basketball practice is a little different.

The big championship game is next week. This is it. It all comes down to this one game and we're all sort of nervous. Even Coach. He's really off his game, having us run drills, then changing his mind and having us run gassers, which is really just us sprinting back and forth on the court. Then he's blowing his whistle again and having us break presses and run fast-break drills.

No one's ever seen Coach this wound up, and he is the most wound-up guy in the school, at least whenever we play against Cedarbrook.

I think we're going to be okay. We really need to just get out there and play.

Billy feels the same way I do. He tells me to relax, which is of course easier said than done. But actually, since I have Miranda in my life and the pressure of trying out for the play, I'm not thinking about basketball every minute of the day, which might be a good thing.

Miranda

To: Tom

From: Miranda

Date: January 11, 2016 8:46 PM

Subject: I Miss You!

Tom,

I can't thank you enough for your words of encouragement last night about the auditions. You were right, I needed to have the right attitude. I was positive and confident and assured. And all because of YOU!

I sang "I'm Not at All in Love" and feel I hit the notes right about where I wanted. There's a seventh-grader who nailed it. But I doubt Mr. Wexler would give her the lead. An eighth-grader deserves the role and I will be confident because that's your advice.

I'm so happy you know so much about theater. You can't believe some of the auditions that I had to sit through! I won't bore you with the details besides telling you the "star" of the basketball team auditioned. He sang "Mary Had a Little

Lamb" because he didn't know anything else.

Ugh! I can't wait to get out of middle school.

Why do you have to be so far away?!

Big big hugs!

Miranda ☺

To: Erica

From: Miranda

Date: January 11, 2016 8:57 PM

Subject: Ugh!!!!!

E

I think today was the worst day of my life. I can't believe I messed up my audition. How could I possibly forget the lyrics?!

BTW—am I crazy or was it totally unfair that Mr. Wexler had Chollie Muller and Sam Dolan audition before the real auditions began?!

I hope you know that you were awesome today. No matter what roles we get I know we're going to have great fun. And we get to make fun of Mr. Wexler's berets!

Also, sorry I haven't been at lunch (science project!) but we'll catch up in the cafeteria tomorrow. I promise.

M ☺

7

The Cast Is Dye

CHOLLIE

Basketball. Basketball. Basketball.

The championship game is next week, and I think we're ready to go. And as I'm walking down the hall I'm dribbling an invisible basketball, keeping my head up and spinning to avoid teachers and students. I can actually hear the roar of the crowd.

So I'm kind of shocked when Sam Dolan grabs my arm as I'm "dribbling" by the main bulletin board. I still have the roar of the crowd in my head, so I don't hear what Sam is saying. But I follow his finger and he's pointing to where they've posted the results of the play tryouts. I can't believe it. I've been so busy I forgot all about the tryouts for the play, and that was only three days ago. Boy, time sure flies when you're having fun.

My name is at the bottom of the list as Second Helper.

"What the heck is the Second Helper?" I ask Sam. His name is on top of mine as First Helper.

"I don't know what it means," Sam says with a big smile, "but if it's on the board, it's gotta be good."

Sam is right. It's really great that I made the play, especially since the whole lab partner thing with Miranda has kind of not worked out. She's one of these workaholic types, so when we're together, it's just work, work, work. But I get it, because whenever I'm practicing football or baseball or basketball, I'm in a zone. That's the way Miranda is with science.

Miranda comes along to see where her name is. It's not on top, which I figure is not a good thing. Sharon Dolan's name is on top. And I think Miranda is upset her name isn't on top. A huge part of me wants to go over to Miranda and tell her it will be okay, but we're just not at that point yet.

Then Miranda goes over to Sharon Dolan and congratulates Sharon for having her name on the top of the list, sort of like shaking hands after a football game. It's all really confusing, this play stuff, but I'm learning.

"Why do you want to be in the play anyway?" Sam asks.

I forget Sam is still standing next to me.

It's weird that Sam wants to know why I want to be in the play. But he's been acting weird lately. I see him at the library almost all the time, which is odd because I always thought Sam was like me and didn't know where the library was.

"A guy can't be too one-dimensional," I tell Sam, dribbling my imaginary ball to science class.

SAM

This morning Sharon is in a rotten mood because she ripped one of her contact lenses and has to wear her glasses.

"Four eyes are better than two," I say, trying to cheer her up.

Sharon holds up a spoon and waves it at me in a threatening manner. "Don't push my buttons. Don't."

I look at Dad and he just goes on eating his toast. And Mom acts like nothing happened.

"Would you like some orange juice, dear?" she asks Sharon, as if she had *not* just threatened me.

So much for trying to lighten the mood.

But you see, this isn't just this morning. When I really think about it, this type of thing happens almost every day before we even get a chance to rub the sleep out of our eyes. The day before, Sharon and Maureen were both mad at Mom because she said something about them not eating enough breakfast.

So now I'm not going to talk to Miranda in the morning, and I'm thinking about avoiding all females before noon.

At school, the day gets a little bit better because for the first time in a while Lichtensteiner doesn't accost me in the hallway. I have to say, who needs bullies when you've got a big lunk like him roaming the halls?

But I'm not letting Lichtensteiner and the toilet paper get me down. And I'm not letting my sisters' erratic behavior in the morning get me down. I'm not letting anything get me down, because I have a play to star in.

Well, I'm not exactly a star, but my name is on the list, second to the bottom, and it says I'm First Helper. Believe it or not, Chollie Muller has got a part, too. When Chollie walks past me, I show him his name. I immediately wish I didn't because for some weird reason, I don't want Chollie Muller in the play.

It sort of burns me up, seeing Chollie's name beneath mine. Not only does he get to work with Miranda Mullaly in science class, but now he's going to be in the play with her, too. And seeing Chollie in the school library working on the science report with Miranda really gets me. I'd bet Chollie didn't even know there was a school library until he started working with Miranda. You can pretty much understand why Chollie is at the bottom of my good-guy list.

Everybody's talking, but I don't say anything to anyone because I don't know anyone in the play all that much. It's really just all the dorks that run for student council and write for the crappy student paper. They're whispering to each other and it doesn't take a genius to tell there's something wrong. Then I realize what the whispering's all about. Sharon's name is on top, next to the part of Babe, and that's the lead. Everyone thought Miranda would get that part, not a seventh-grader.

Then everyone quiets down as Miranda Mullaly comes up with Erica Dickerson in tow. Geez, I wish Erica Dickerson would go away. I can't even congratulate Miranda because Erica is at her side like a bodyguard. Erica must be related to Lichtensteiner.

Then Sharon comes along and sees her name up on top and does her best not to act too excited. But I know Sharon. I'll be hearing about this all night at dinner and all night when I'm trying to watch television. But like I said, Sharon plays it cool, kind of lifts her eyebrows as if she's surprised, and then Miranda comes up to Sharon and they talk for a couple of seconds. Then Miranda shakes Sharon's hand. It's really funny, all this showbiz stuff. It's like they all have their own little world and their own little rules.

So as I'm walking off to class, thinking about Miranda, I let my guard down and walk right into Lichtensteiner.

"Where you going, Dolan?" he asks, apparently unaware we're in a school.

"To class."

"Where's your class?"

"Biology, and I don't want to be late."

"Have you been to the bathroom yet today?" Lichtensteiner asks, just like it's a normal question. God, this school is really horrible sometimes.

"Isn't that a little personal?"

Lichtensteiner has to think about this, he really does.

"All right, Dolan, don't be late."

I don't even bother saying anything else. If I didn't have basketball and the play and Miranda Mullaly, I would really go off on Mr. Lichtensteiner and tell him what I really think about his nose hairs and how he runs the school and how he should invest in a toothbrush. But I have a lot going on and can't worry about Lichtensteiner's toilet paper problem.

In science class Duke comes up to me, rocking back and forth on his feet, and starts talking to me about the play, just like we're old buddies.

"So, Sam, I see you're in the play," he says.

"Yup," I say.

"I look forward to working with you," Duke says, but it kind of seems like he's lying.

"Yup," I repeat, hoping he gets the idea that I don't want to talk to him.

"Of course," he goes on, "I have the lead and you're only First Helper."

I'm not liking the way Duke is talking about this, like

he's better than me, if you know what I mean. But I keep my cool.

"The cast is dye," I tell Duke. I'm not sure what this means, but I know I've heard it before and I know enough to know that I'm in the cast.

It works, too, because Duke, the weirdo, gets a confused look on his face and doesn't know what to say and finally leaves.

Duke

The roles for the spring musical were due to be posted on the bulletin board outside the main office. But before I took a peek at how Mr. Wexler would ruin this year's show, I decided to toss a bit of toilet paper in the bathroom next to the computer lab. I did my job and left behind Sam's math work that I picked out of the trash can yesterday.

I was in a jolly good mood knowing Mr. Lichtensteiner would pester Sam Dolan before the morning was over, and I was so sure I would be playing opposite Miranda Mullaly that I was practically floating down the corridor. So you can imagine my surprise when the first thing I see above my name is DOLAN, and then I look over to see Sam Dolan smiling. I almost collapsed.

Was I unaware of some demented interpretation of *The Pajama Game*? Was Babe going to be Sam Dolan in drag? Don't laugh. There's little I would put past Mr. Wexler when trying to attract an audience for the musical. But then I saw Sam congratulate his sister Sharon, who gave quite a performance at the audition. She must have been adopted.

I gathered my strength and stood up straight, steady on my feet after seeing my hopes of costarring with Miranda crushed. And then I saw Miranda's name below mine and below Sharon's, across from the role of Gladys.

Miranda, bless her soul, looked a little shocked. Erica Dickerson, who was cast as the stupid secretary, Mabel, told her to cheer up. Gladys, I must admit, is a meaty role, maybe even as good as the role of Babe.

Out of the corner of my eye, I saw Chollie Muller getting a high five from Ralph Waldo because Chollie is Second Helper. Lord save us if he has to speak. And above Chollie's name was Sam Dolan's as First Helper. At least he didn't get a better part than that.

I'd seen enough and left for class.

In science, I struck up a little conversation with Sam in order to find out his intentions regarding the show. Sherlock Holmes would have needed to put on a costume to hide his identity, but for a knucklehead like Sam, there was no need to bother beating around the bush. And for the first time in my life, I felt sorry for the teachers at Penn Valley. What a heartbreaking waste of time it is to try to educate imbeciles like Sam. He actually said, "The cast is die"[14] with a pathetic righteous indignation as if he actu-

---

14. What he meant to say is "the die is cast," in reference to Julius Caesar's famous crossing of the Rubicon River in 49 BC.

ally knew what he was talking about. I would normally feel sorry for Sam, but because of the thumbtack and his penchant for hovering around Miranda, he is my enemy and I am his.

Miranda

To: Erica
From: Miranda
Date: January 14, 2016 9:02 PM
Subject: Gladys

E,

I just got off the phone with the world's greatest boyfriend and I feel so much better about the role of Gladys. Tom agreed with you that I shouldn't let it get me down not getting the lead. After all, it's only a middle school musical.

I'm sorry for being such a weirdo about it today. It's just that I had my heart set on the lead. Thanks for being there and cheering me up.

Isn't it amazing that I have the world's best boyfriend and the world's best friend? I don't know what I would do without you two.

XOXOXO

M ☺

Freewriting

Duke Vanderbilt Samagura

18 January 2016

English 8A

Mr. Minkin

Suggested Writing Prompt: *Where do you see yourself in five years? What will your life look like? What important relationships will be in your life? Explain.*

Sir:

Have you ever heard of Harvard University? That's where I'll be in five years.

And you, sir, will still be here at Penn Valley Middle School, giving students stupid writing prompts and ripping off the taxpayers.

I can picture myself now, crossing Harvard Yard on my way to a lecture on intellectual history or maybe Russian novelists. On my arm will be Miranda Mullaly, and we'll be laughing at our memories from our senior prom and, possibly, even sharing a couple of laughs about Penn Valley Middle School. Perhaps something about how stupid the teachers are.

"Doesn't it all seem so long ago?" Miranda will ask.

"It all seems to be a dream, looking back on it now," I will say, squeezing her hand.

Miranda will walk me to my classroom and there we will part for only an hour. Miranda will promise me she will read her art history text and not miss me too much. I will promise Miranda I will meet her after class on the steps of the Widener Library. (Did you know the library at Harvard is called the Harry Elkins Widener Memorial Library? Now you know. Good for you, Mr. Minkin, you're learning something.)

And all this will happen despite the handicap of having had Robert Minkin as my eighth-grade English teacher.

Sam Dolan

January 18th

English 8A

Mr. Minkin

Suggested Writing Prompt: *Where do you see yourself in five years? What will your life look like? What important relationships will be in your life? Explain.*

Hey Mr. Minkin,

Another great question. I am really enjoying these writing prompts.

And five years is a good future time to think about. It's going to be great in five years. I'll finally be out of school and have my chance to move to New York or Los Angeles (wherever Miranda ends up) to start my career as a professional funny person. Maybe doing standup about my sisters or doing stunts for funny movies. I decided to turn "Watch This!" into a book and it's already way better than the stuff Johnny Knoxville comes up with. Someone should pay me for it!

Dad and I have talked about it but I made him

promise he wouldn't tell Mom. I know she'll say I should go to college. It's not like I have anything against college. I mean, I'm sure it's great for some guys but I just imagine college with a whole bunch of dorks like Duke Samagura carrying around briefcases and wearing sports jackets. Besides, I don't want to waste any time. I just want to get out there and make people laugh.

An awesome question, once again, Mr. Minkin!

Chollie Muller

January 18, 2015

English 8A

Mr. Minkin

Suggested Writing Prompt: *Where do you see yourself in five years? What will your life look like? What important relationships will be in your life? Explain.*

Dear Mr. Minkin,

Are we going to be in high school in five years?

If so, I'm hoping I'll be on the basketball team and we'll be in the middle of a great season.

And I'm hoping Billy gets back on his feet and gets a job or goes back to school.

And then, most importantly, if all goes as planned, I'll be preparing for the prom with Miranda Mullaly. I'll have a license by then and I'll borrow Dad's car and I'll rent a tuxedo and Miranda will wear a pretty dress and I'll say "Holy Moley!" and Billy will be super impressed as Miranda and I drive off for the prom.

So that's where I plan to be in five years. In high school, on the basketball team, with Miranda Mullaly as my girlfriend.

The future looks bright!

Miranda Mullaly

January 18, 2016

English 8A

Mr. Minkin

Suggested Writing Prompt: *Where do you see yourself in five years? What will your life look like? What important relationships will be in your life? Explain.*

I don't want to get ahead of myself, but I can see Tom and me in the future, holding hands walking across a tree-lined college campus. I'm thinking Williams or Amherst, or maybe Swarthmore, if we decide to stay closer to home. We'll both have books under our arms; Tom will probably study Economics, I just know it! I'll probably have about ten worn and dog-eared paperbacks, doing my research for my thesis on Jane Austen.

Tom and I will sit down under an elm tree, or maybe a chestnut. Of course we'll have a blanket and there will be apples and all the other students will pass by us and wish they had the love we have. Professors will pass us and think to themselves, ah, youth!

Or, maybe we'll be in a train station in Paris. We'll carry all our belongings and guidebooks stuffed in our backpacks. And we'll have a year together in Europe, getting lost on cobblestone streets, eating too much pastry, and learning new languages before we begin college. Secretly, I hope we'll do the latter.

Either way, I just can't wait!

9

The Championship Game

CHOLLIE

After I miss the two free throws at the end of the championship game today I'm just about sick to my stomach. But when I look around the locker room, no one else seems to care as much. In fact, Coach is the only one really upset about the game. I *feel* like crying, but Coach is *actually* crying. It's really weird. And with Coach sobbing across from me, I feel worse because this is how he reacted after I fumbled the ball going in for a touchdown against Cedarbrook in the fall.

I know I shouldn't care, but I still feel bad about it because I feel responsible. I should've made those two shots at the end of the game.

It's just killing me inside. I have been waiting forever for this game. And not only do I want to win it for myself because Cedarbrook beats us in everything, but I also want to win it for Miranda.

The gym is so crowded that the cheerleaders have to sit underneath the baskets because there isn't any room on the bleachers. Can you believe that? It's just like a college game.

The first half isn't too bad because the cheerleaders are on the end where we play defense so I can't see them. But in the second half we're shooting right where they are. I try to block it out of my head, I really do, but then I figure I'll just play harder for Miranda. And it works. We hold the lead at the end of the third quarter. But then Sam Dolan misses a layup when he is all alone, and we have a couple of turnovers, and Cedarbrook crawls right back into the game.

And here's the part that makes me sick. We are down one point (one point!) and we have the ball. Coach calls a time-out and we're standing around him, waiting for him to draw up the play. Then out of the corner of my eye, I see Miranda with the cheerleaders doing their final cheer for us and I take charge.

"I can beat my man, Coach," I say.

Coach looks at me like he's never seen me before. He

looks really stressed, like he can't talk, so he nods and gives me the drawing board.

So I get right to it.

"Okay, now, we have eight seconds. I'll take the in-bounds pass and we'll clear out the lane. Sam, you drive to the basket. If your guy comes up to stop me, you'll be wide open underneath the basket."

The horn blows and we break the huddle.

Everything happens so fast. I beat my guy and drive down the lane and Sam's guy comes up to me but I can't get the pass off to him. The next thing I know, I'm on the ground and the crowd's cheering and the ref tells me I get two free throws.

At the free throw line, I look straight down at my sneakers, because I know if I look up, I'll see Miranda Mullaly. But I have to look up so I can see the basket. I do and there's Miranda, her pom-poms under her chin, really interested in what will happen next. I know it's stupid, but I just smile at Miranda. A big smile. A smile like I've already made the shots and we won the game.

Then I go on and miss both free throws and we lose the game because of me.

And that's why Coach is crying in the locker room after the game.

Last year I probably would've been crying along with Coach. And I do feel bad about losing. But I'm also happy because I get to see Miranda Mullaly tonight at the library so we can finish our report on the Brazilian tapir.

I must be going crazy.

SAM

Picture this. It's the championship game and it's the final seconds and I'm open under the basket. Can you picture it? I'm all alone under the basket. So all I need is for Chollie Muller to make the pass—the pass *he* draws up during the time-out—so I can put the ball in the basket and we can win the championship.

It's not that difficult, right?

And the best part is Miranda Mullaly is practically right under the basket. So I get to be the hero and Miranda Mullaly gets to jump in my arms and the whole school gets to pour out of the bleachers and do a victory dance at center court.

But none of this happens. None of this happens because Chollie Muller, the fathead, decides to shoot when he's got two Cedarbrook players draped over him. Lucky for Chollie, the ref calls a foul. So now all Chollie has to do is make the two free throws and we win.

We line up and the gym is pretty quiet, and I look at Chollie, then down at my feet to make sure I don't get a lane violation. Then I look at Chollie again and you'll never believe what I see. Chollie isn't looking at the rim and concentrating on his shot, but instead is looking at Miranda Mullaly. I'm not making this up.

Well, of course, Chollie misses the first shot because he's not even looking at the basket. Unbelievable.

Then it gets even quieter, if that's possible. Chollie bends his knees and looks like he's going to make the shot, and we'll at least have overtime. *Clank!* Right off the rim, and we lose.

It's ugly in the locker room after the game. Like all of the teachers at Penn Valley, Coach is a nut job. He's actually crying. It's kind of weird watching a grown man cry over a basketball game, it really is. And then as he's sitting there he grabs one of my socks and starts wiping his nose with it.

So I leave the locker room with only one sock, and we lost the big game, and now I know that Chollie Muller has got a thing for Miranda Mullaly. And I have to meet up with Erica Dickerson at the library tonight. And my mom is going to yell at me because I only have one sock (I don't want to touch my other one because Coach's snot is all over it). If anybody should be crying, it should be me.

Duke

Thanks to Neal and Cassandra having used my upbringing as a sociological experiment, I know basketball.

When I was eight, I was the point guard for the Immaculate Conception Cougars.

When I was nine, I played the two (shooting guard) for Beth Shalom synagogue.

When I was ten and a few inches taller, I played power forward for the Penn Valley United Methodist church.

When I was eleven, I centered a scrappy and surprisingly sprightly team for the Penn Valley Zendo.[15]

When I was twelve, Neal and Cassandra finished their religious studies. And thus came to an end both my basketball career and my game of theological musical chairs. If they had ever asked me, I would have told them I wanted to keep on playing. I was also rather enjoying my unorthodox religious journey. But alas, they never asked.

The point is, I know basketball. I know a zone defense, the importance of the pressure on the ball, how to block

....

15. A Japanese "meditation hall." In Zen Buddhism, the *zen-dō* is a spiritual dōjō where *zazen* (sitting meditation) is practiced.

passing lanes, and why it's important for the point guard to penetrate on offense.

What I witnessed in the gym this afternoon was hardly basketball. It was a bunch of poorly prepared and solipsistic[16] Penn Valley eighth-graders disgracing both themselves and Penn Valley Middle School. I only went to the game so I could write the following report for the school newspaper:

MULLER SNATCHES DEFEAT
FROM THE JAWS OF VICTORY
Eagles Lose Championship Again

by Duke Vanderbilt Samagura (Sports Editor)

With the game on the line and the championship in sight, Charles "Chollie" Muller missed two free throws with no time remaining, sealing the fate of the Golden Eagles and ending the season short of the championship.

The Eagles played their hearts out against a well-coached and seasoned Wildcats team from rival Cedarbrook. The Eagles jumped off to a quick

---

16. The philosophical idea that the only thing that exists and is real is what one experiences oneself. Not a flattering adjective.

start, leading the Wildcats by four at the end of the first quarter. The Wildcats, however, gamely fought back and took the lead after Muller committed two turnovers and missed three straight shots. At the end of the first half, the teams were knotted at twenty-six.

The Eagles again jumped out to a quick start, leading by six halfway through the third quarter. But once again Muller had difficulty on both ends of the court, putting forth a lackluster effort on defense and missing an uncontested layup.

At the start of the fourth and final quarter, the Eagles and Wildcats traded leads. It was with the final seconds ticking off the clock that Muller drove to the basket, not seeing his open teammates, and tried to win the game on his own. Fortunately for Muller, he was fouled on the play and, with no time left on the clock, was awarded two free throws and the chance at redemption.

But alas, Muller, who appeared to be distracted, missed both free throws. The Cedarbrook players celebrated, while the Eagles left the court losers, undoubtedly wondering how Muller failed to pass the ball and then missed two free throws. It was a difficult defeat for the team, which had worked so hard and showed so much promise, to accept.

I had no trouble writing the above article. In fact, I probably didn't even have to show up. Chollie Muller is always guaranteed to come up short, whether it's missing the free throws at the end of the basketball game or fumbling the winning touchdown in a football game. It will be interesting to see how he messes up during baseball season.

It was difficult, however, to sit in the stands and watch Miranda Mullaly cheer for Chollie and Sam. Although I'm sure she's only a cheerleader to pad her resume for college applications, watching her shake the pom-poms every time we scored a basket was heartrending. Miranda and I should've been onstage together, running through lines and rehearsing our duets, instead of cheering for and reporting on the pathetic basketball team.

10

The Library

Duke

One of the many crosses I have to bear in this world is Neal and Cassandra inviting their university students over for a seminar[17] and pizza. Every graduate student in sociology whom I have ever met is afflicted with some type of disease that makes them pat me on the head and say I'm "cute." You would think college students would have a better vocabulary, or at the very least, the ability to recognize my superior intellect.

Needless to say, I was a fugitive and had nowhere to

----

17. A small classroom meeting designed not as a lecture but where each student is given a chance to speak about the assigned readings.

go but the library. At least there I could curl up with a *New Yorker* (the pages are always pristine—not very flattering for my hometown). The library, since it contains books, is usually empty.

So how bad could it be? A couple of hours in a quiet library. I was actually looking forward to a relaxing, low-stress evening. It also would give me a chance to contemplate what I would write in Miranda's Valentine's candy-gram.

But such nights are not to be had at Penn Valley. The first person I saw upon entering the library was Sam Dolan. He surprisingly had a book in his hands that he was, *not* surprisingly, holding upside down. I suspect he was waiting for his lab partner, Erica Dickerson. I can't stand Erica. She's like a female Sam Dolan with an IQ in the double digits. I have noticed, however, Erica spending a lot of time with Miranda, so I should probably be nice to her just in case Miranda asks her what she thinks about me.

I passed the half-wit without being seen, grabbed the untouched *New Yorker*, and took a seat at a table that had two bookshelves protecting me from Sam. I began to read an article about the President of NYU[18] when I heard *her* voice.

....

18. New York University, located in Manhattan. (I may study film there in graduate school for a lark.)

Sinking lower into my seat, I waited like the proverbial dumb blonde in a horror movie.

And then, much to my despair, Chollie and Miranda passed by my table.

Chollie, of course, saw me out of the corner of his eye. "Hiya, Duke."

I could only nod. You're not supposed to talk in the library anyway.

Miranda took a chair at the table next to mine. But Chollie just stood in front of me, a stupid smile on his stupid face.

And since Nikki Shepherd had decided she wanted to do her science report alone and I was already finished with my newspaper article, I had no choice but to pack up my things and go home.

It's hard to describe how upsetting it was to have my little place of peace disturbed by the likes of Chollie Muller and Sam Dolan.

I tried to sneak up to my room to avoid the seminar. Unfortunately, a student caught me in the hallway when I wasn't looking and tousled my hair and called me cute. Too bad I'm too old to kick sociology majors in the shins. I would have enjoyed that.

After I finally escaped, I locked the door to my room, sat down at my desk, looked up at my poster of the Bard,[19] and got to work on writing a note for the candy-gram I would send to Miranda on Valentine's Day.

I wrote out about fifty different cards but couldn't settle on exactly what I wanted to say. At some point I ran out of gas and slept at my desk until Cassandra and Neal rudely woke me and carried me to bed.

19. The inimitable poet and playwright William Shakespeare. When I finally have some free time, I intend to commit my favorite sonnets to memory.

CHOLLIE

I'm especially excited to see Miranda at the library tonight because I'm going to talk to her about the Valentine's Day dance. Billy thinks it's a good idea to strike up a conversation about the dance so she won't be surprised when I ask her to go with me. I know it's still weeks away, but Billy says a girl like Miranda will have lots of guys lining up to ask her.

But here's what actually happens at the library.

I get there early before Miranda shows up, and I have all my stuff out because I know Miranda likes to get right to work. Then I wait for Miranda at the door so I can be a gentleman and hold it open and all that stuff.

Miranda's dad drops her off and I make small talk, which is not one of my strongest points. And of course I really can't remember what I said, because I was nervous. But I know I didn't say anything stupid because I always remember when I say something dumb.

Miranda leads the way (the librarian knows her name and says hello to her, which I think is awesome) and we take our seats at the table I saved for us. Duke Samagura is at the next table, and I say hi to him to be polite and show good manners, but Duke scurries away like there's a fire. He's a weird dude sometimes.

Then Miranda gets right to work. It's amazing. She's got the whole report on her computer and a rough draft with handwritten notes, and it sort of makes me feel like I haven't done a lot of work. So as Miranda's typing away, I pretend I have notes to read through and something to add, but I really just wait to mention the Valentine's Day dance.

I have no idea how much time passes as I sit there just trying to get the guts to even talk about the dance. It's much worse than standing at the free throw line. Finally I look up from my papers.

"Miranda," a voice says.

But it's not my voice. It's Erica Dickerson's voice. And before I know it, Erica is standing right beside me talking to Miranda about who knows what.

And then they're laughing, but I don't know what they're laughing about, so I just go along and laugh with them and I really feel stupid. I don't know what's going on.

When it's all said and done, I don't say anything to Miranda about the dance, and the report is all finished, and there's nothing to do but say good night and go home. This really bums me out because now that the report is finished, we won't have any reason to go to the library, and I didn't say anything about the Valentine's dance.

What a terrible end to a terrible day.

SAM

Erica Dickerson is late meeting me at the library to work on our science report. Miranda is never late, so I end up having to watch her walk by with Chollie Muller and set up camp a few tables away. It just drives me nuts, seeing Chollie with her, especially after watching him look into Miranda's eyes at the basketball game today. And then lucky Chollie gets to work with her in the library tonight of all nights. I wish I had a thumbtack waiting on his seat.

To take my mind off this, I pull out a book I'm borrowing from my mom called *I Feel Bad About My Neck* by Nora Ephron. It's supposed to be "thoughts on being a woman," but I'm really not getting much out of it besides learning that New York City is expensive and most skin creams that women use to combat aging don't work. But my mom laughed out loud when she read it, so I thought I'd give it a try. To me, though, the book is very disappointing and not really funny. It's probably the kind of book Erica Dickerson would write.

"Thoughts on being a woman," Erica Dickerson says, and before I know it, she has the book in her hands. "What, are you planning on becoming a woman someday?" If it weren't for her bad manners, she wouldn't have any manners at all.

"You know, that's really rude, taking my book out of my hands like that," I say.

"Oh, I'm sorry," she says with a lot of sarcasm as she takes a seat across from me.

I grab the book back and hide it in my bag.

"You know what's a really great book?"

"No," I say. "What's a really great book?" And I'm being very sarcastic.

"*Twilight*," she says, which is really nothing new to me because my sister Maureen has about fifteen copies of those books. They're everywhere in the house.

"*Twilight*, huh?" I say, and I take out all my yak stuff so Erica Dickerson gets the idea that I'm ready to finish this report and go home.

"Oh yeah, it's my favorite book. And Miranda's, too."

This last piece of information really gets my attention.

"*Twilight*, eh?"

So I write "Twilight!!!!!!" on my list of things to do.

Knowing this energizes me. So now I'm ready to start this report so I can get home and start reading *Twilight*. But Erica Dickerson has other plans.

"I'll be right yak," she says.

"What?"

"I'll be right *yak*."

"What are you talking about?"

"Think about it, Dolan. I'll be right *yak.*"

Erica actually laughs at her own stupid joke. She also calls her backpack her back*yak* or *yak*pack. Just when I'm getting along with her, she has to go and say something unfunny like that.

Before I even get a chance to tell her as much, she runs off to talk to Miranda. And then I can hear them laughing and I have this terrible feeling they are laughing at me. Even Chollie Muller is laughing.

I can't wait for this day to end.

11

Give Me Toilet Paper!

SAM

Picture this. I walk into school just minding my own business, you see, because I'm in a bad mood. My book bag weighs about a thousand pounds because I have all the Twilight books in it, I have rehearsals for the musical after school, and I still have no idea how I'm going to move along my relationship with Miranda Mullaly. I'm a man with a lot on his mind.

But Lichtensteiner has finally had enough of the toilet paper tossing in the bathroom and decides to take all the paper from the boys' bathrooms. And then he goes around telling everybody to ask *me* about it. Like I've been saying all along, I'm not the one who's tossing the toilet paper. I don't even go in the dirty boys' room, since Coach opens the locker room for the basketball players. It's a really big perk of being on the team.

Anyway, Lichtensteiner takes all the toilet paper from the boys' rooms today and doesn't say anything. Some guys find out too late, if you know what I mean. You can actually hear people screaming for help from the bathroom. And somehow, within minutes, Tony Worthington is selling Kleenex Pocket Packs out of the school store at a steep markup.

By lunchtime all the kids, at least the guys, are just about going nuts, and everybody's asking *me* what the deal is. I've never been in a riot before but I certainly can see how they can start.

No one wants to eat their lunch and all people can think about is going to the bathroom. And I'm wondering if I'm safe or if Lichtensteiner has taken the goods from the locker room, too.

Everyone gathers around my lunch table and people are talking about attacking the school office and grabbing the toilet paper or swiping the janitor's keys and looting the supply closet. Matt Vesci talks about leaving a little present outside Lichtensteiner's door. Am I making myself clear? We are just about to have a revolution.

So I get up on a chair and I explain that I have nothing to do with the whole thing. I think everyone believes me, which puts my mind at ease because this group is getting scary. But as I'm up on the chair explaining myself, I start thinking about how Lichtensteiner is blaming the toilet paper throwing on me and it gets me worked up.

Next thing I know, I'm giving a speech. I say things like "Toilet paper's a right" and might even throw in something about all men being created equal. Anyway, I end the thing by screaming the funniest thing I can think to say to this mob, "Give me toilet paper, or give me death!"

Those words really get everyone going. We storm out of the cafeteria and head toward the office, when I remember there's a student council meeting going on.

We burst through the auditorium doors and crash the meeting.

Duke Samagura bangs his gavel, like that's really going to stop us. Mr. Porter, who is a decent guy but needs to do something about his dandruff, stops us, though to tell the truth we don't have anywhere else to go.

He wants to know what's going on.

I let him have it, trying to remember all the history he has taught me. I don't know if I got the natural rights of man correct, or if I did, I don't know if I tied it to toilet paper properly. But when I end it with "Give us toilet paper, or give us death!" I get another round of applause. Boy, that's a heck of a line.

Mr. Porter calms us down a bit and finally processes the entire toilet paper spiel. He takes me by the arm and the two of us go to the main office. Mr. Porter goes into Mr. Lichtensteiner's office and comes out about a minute later with rolls and rolls of toilet paper.

We walk back down the aisle to the auditorium with rolls falling from our arms. I start throwing the toilet paper, and everyone else starts to throw it around, too. We're all going wild and before I know it, I'm up on some dude's shoulders and I'm just about the biggest hero in the world. And a comedy legend.

I toss the toilet paper and a couple of guys run out with it, laughing and crying tears of joy. It's the happiest we've ever been at Penn Valley.

And I just know Lichtensteiner said to the teachers, "Watch this," as he pulled the toilet paper from the bathrooms. He is going get an honorable mention when *Watch This!* is published.

CHOLLIE

When I got home from the library two weeks ago, Billy didn't even ask me how it went with Miranda. Instead, he waved a newspaper in front of me.

"Here it is," Billy says, waving the newspaper. "Here's your ticket to your lady friend's heart."

"A newspaper?"

"No, no, no," Billy says, handing me the paper. "Right there on the front page."

I read the first couple of paragraphs, and it's about how the ocean is going to rise up and swallow a bunch of cities and flood everything, and everything is going to be really rotten and horrible. They call it global warming, and I think one of my teachers told us about it, but I can't really be sure.

"So you think Miranda will be interested in this?" I ask.

"You have to bring it up at your student council meeting."

"Billy, we don't pass laws and things like that."

"What you have to do is give a speech about it, then you say you want to petition Congress and the president. If this Miranda is the kind of girl I think she is, she'll eat this up, and before you know it, you and Miranda will be partnered up to stop global warming."

Well, I take Billy's advice and we work together on a pretty big speech about the globe and climate and rain and the sun and just about everything you can imagine. Last night we put the finishing touches on it and by the time we're done it's pretty late but I'm so excited I can hardly sleep.

And then when I get to school I'm so nervous about the speech I keep feeling like I have to go to the bathroom. But of course, just my luck, there's no toilet paper in the boys' room.

So that's why I'm really nervous standing in front of the student council about to give a big speech. Maybe even more nervous than when I took the foul shots. But when I look at Miranda and see her waiting to hear what I have to say, with her big brown eyes smiling at me, well, I feel like I can do just about anything. Even if I do have to go to the bathroom.

And then, just as I'm about to speak, I mean right after I clear my throat, I hear a lot of noise coming from outside the auditorium.

"Ladies and gentlemen," I begin. And then I smile right at Miranda and say, "Madam President." But Miranda is looking at the door. Everyone is. The noise is getting louder. And then we hear people chanting.

I start over again and *bang!* The auditorium doors fly

open and in comes Sam Dolan and about thirty other guys. They're chanting something about toilet paper.

Well, that's the end of my speech and the end of the student council meeting. By the time things come to order, Mr. Porter leaves with Sam Dolan, and I look around but can't find Miranda Mullaly.

Duke

My only purpose at the student council meeting today is to schedule when Miranda and I will meet to finalize plans and put on the final touches for the Valentine's Day dance. It's only nine days away and I can't wait.

But nothing works according to plan. As Jonathan Swift[20] wrote, "When a true genius appears in the world, you may know him by this sign; that the dunces are all in confederacy against him." In this instance, yours truly is the genius, and Mr. Lichtensteiner, Penn Valley's poor excuse for a vice principal, is one of far too many dunces.

The meeting started when Chollie Muller asked for the floor so he could address the student council about a most pressing issue, an issue apparently keeping him up at night. And just as Chollie was to open his speech, he was interrupted by Sam Dolan and a group of ne'er-do-wells and hooligans complaining about toilet paper.

I jumped from my seat and banged my gavel, preparing to protect Miranda, our president. Mr. Porter took Sam and left the auditorium. The rest of the rabble continued to

20. The great Irish writer and satirist most famous for his masterpiece *Gulliver's Travels.*

chant that they wanted toilet paper or death, thus making a farce of Patrick Henry's[21] important speech.

As the mob continued its "demonstration," I turned to Miranda to confirm our plans for the dance and I could see in her eyes she was demoralized, distraught, and disgusted. This is public education for you. I summoned Knuckles and Moose to stand between Miranda and me and the mob.

By the time Mr. Porter returned, there was toilet paper for everyone. Sam was carried out on the mob's shoulders like a hero, and toilet paper was flying through the air.

Silence descended upon the room when they left. Chollie was still standing at podium, looking as confused as ever.

Mr. Porter looked at his watch.

"I guess that's all the time we have for today."

21. Patrick Henry, an important American revolutionary, demanded in a speech to the Virginia Convention, "Give me liberty, or give me death."

Miranda

Mr. Porter
History Teacher
Penn Valley Middle School

Dear Mr. Porter,

What occurred this afternoon at the student council meeting was beneath the standards of this or any student council. As president of the Penn Valley Middle School student council, I am entrusted by the student body to look after their best interests and propose ideas to improve the school and the learning environment. The outburst at the meeting this afternoon, and your reaction to it, was disappointing.

You may find such occurrences acceptable. You may even find such outrageous behavior funny. I, however, do not.

I hereby resign my position of student council
president, effective immediately.

Regards,

Miranda Mullaly

Miranda Mullaly

To: Erica

From: Miranda

Date: February 3, 2016 8:43 PM

Subject: What was that?

_____

E,

I've decided that I'm finished with the student council. I just
wrote a resignation letter to Mr. Porter (which I'll probably
have to read to him!).

Anyway, after the toilet paper thing today I've just had
enough. And this gives me a perfect chance to get out of the
Valentine's dance check-in, which I still hadn't told him I was
not going to do.

Here's what I won't miss:

- Looking at the dandruff fall from Mr. Porter's hair and
  beard.
- Being in yet another room with Duke Samagura.
- Being the only one (besides you!) to work on any of the
  projects we sometimes get around to doing.
- Setting up for dances.

Here's what I will miss:

• Nothing! Hah!!

See you tomorrow!

M☺

PS Can't wait for the dance!

12

Freewriting

Sam Dolan

February 11th (almost Valentine's!)

English 8A

Mr. Minkin

Suggested Writing Prompt: *What event are you most looking forward to in the next year? It could be as far away as a year or as soon as tomorrow. Why is this occasion so important to you? How can you best prepare yourself for this event? Explain.*

Hey Mr. Minkin,

    This is a great question. And there sure are a lot of things I'm looking forward to. I know this is a writing assignment, but I have to write out a list because I have so many exciting things coming up in my near future:

1. The Valentine's Day dance
2. The spring musical
3. Summer break. Hopefully Foxxy won't spend every second with Holly Culver.
4. Starting high school (and not having to see Lichtensteiner every day!)
5. Not having to do writing prompts—only kidding!

Before I get into the dance (which is what I'm most looking forward to) you should also know I'm pretty excited about the musical. Who would've thought it could be so much fun? I've never been into singing and dancing except as a joke, but it really ain't so bad. I even like some of the songs. For being old and all, they have pretty catchy melodies and I can't get them out of my head.

And then there's the number I'm going to do with Miranda Mullaly called "Steam Heat." We haven't started working on the dance steps but Miss Kerrigan says it's one of the biggest scenes in the whole show. So I got that going for me.

This brings me to the really big event I'm looking forward to: the Valentine's Day dance.

I have it all planned to dance with Miranda

when there's a slow song. I'm kind of bummed
that I have to go with my sister, but at least I
know I won't be late because Sharon is one of
these people who plans everything ahead.

And here's the best part. I know Miranda is
excited to go to the dance because she told me
yesterday. I haven't been talking to her a lot in
the morning because I know how miserable girls
are at that time and she probably isn't in the
mood to talk. And every time I do get a chance
to strike up a conversation, Erica Dickerson
comes along and sticks her nose in. But yesterday
I saw Miranda all alone at rehearsal and I chatted
her up.

For the first time I felt confident about talking
to Miranda. Because of Sharon, I now know
how to talk properly about the theater. You
say "musical" or "show" instead of "play." And
"Steam Heat" is a number and not a scene. And
you don't practice like a sport. You rehearse. So
I was very excited to talk with Miranda, if you
know what I mean.

She was waiting at the side of the stage (stage
left if you're a theater person) watching Duke and
Sharon go through their dance steps.

Me: Hiya.
Miranda: Hello.
Me: This is really fun, isn't it?
Miranda: Yes.
Me: I'm really glad I'm in the musical this year.
Miranda: Uh huh.
Me: That was some kind of student council meeting last week, wasn't it?
Miranda: It wasn't what I expected, if that's what you mean.
Me: (Pause) I guess life is kind of unpredictable.
(Miranda huffs at this, the way Lichtensteiner does. I quickly change the subject.)
Me: The Valentine's Day dance should be fun, heh?
(Miranda turns to me and smiles.)
Miranda: Oh, I can't wait for the dance.

When you add that I've finished the first Twilight book and will have plenty to talk about with Miranda, yeah, you can say I am really looking forward to the dance.

And so is Miranda Mullaly!

Duke Vanderbilt Samagura

11 February 2016

English 8A

Mr. Minkin

Suggested Writing Prompt: *What event are you most looking forward to in the next year? It could be as far away as a year or as soon as tomorrow. Why is this occasion so important to you? How can you best prepare yourself for this event? Explain.*

Sir:

Obviously I'm most looking forward to not having to waste my time on your inane writing prompts.

That said, I'm actually looking forward to a few things, which is rare in this emporium of mindlessness known as Penn Valley Middle School.

Let me indulge you.

I am looking forward to <u>The Pajama Game</u>.

I am looking forward to leaving Penn Valley.

I was also looking forward to the Valentine's Day dance but now, thanks to Miranda's resignation, I will not be working the door with her. Now I have to rely on a candy-gram to appropriately express my feelings and set the tone for the dance.

And now I have to work alone with your vapid colleague, Mr. Porter, who will probably bring his bore of a wife.

Chollie Muller
February 11, 2015
English 8A
Mr. Minkin

Suggested Writing Prompt: *What event are you most looking forward to in the next year? It could be as far away as a year or as soon as tomorrow. Why is this occasion so important to you? How can you best prepare yourself for this event? Explain.*

Dear Mr. Minkin,

I'm really looking forward to the Valentine's Day dance this Friday.

I'm so lucky I have my awesome big brother to help me, too. We have a whole plan for the night.

You know how they split the gym in half with the partitions so you can either play basketball or dance? Well, last Halloween I played so much basketball I hardly even knew there was a party going on. And I didn't even get any pizza!

But this time there will be no basketball. In fact, Billy has been coaching and preparing me. He has even given me a list of songs to ask the

DJ to play. About halfway into the evening, I'm going to ask him to play "Stairway to Heaven" and then ask Miranda Mullaly to dance with me.

Billy also says not to talk during the song, which is a really good thing because I think I would stutter if I had to talk and dance at the same time.

And then there's a tricky part with the song, because it starts off slow and then speeds up. Billy says to just sway my hips a little during the fast part and everything should be fine.

I'm also looking forward to the pizza at the dance.

And eventually baseball season.

I know this sounds crazy, but I'm sort of looking forward to the play ending. It's crazy because I wanted to be in it so much. But now that I'm in it, I'm practically having a heart attack every day. I only have one stupid line to say and I can't remember it. And I'm really not much of a singer and they want me to sing a line during this "Hernando's Hideaway" thing. And I hardly get to see Miranda Mullaly during the play practices. So it's all sort of a mess.

Anyway, I guess I can just say I'm looking forward to the dance tomorrow night. It's my big chance and with Billy's help, nothing can go wrong.

Miranda Mullaly

February 11, 2016

English 8A

Mr. Minkin

Suggested Writing Prompt: *What event are you most looking forward to in the next year? It could be as far away as a year or as soon as tomorrow. Why is this occasion so important to you? How can you best prepare yourself for this event? Explain.*

Besides leaving Penn Valley forever, I am, believe it or not, most looking forward to performing in the spring musical. At first, I must admit, I was terribly upset about not getting the lead. When I saw Sharon Dolan's name up on the board I did everything in my power to keep from crying. But now as I watch Duke Samagura order Sharon around, and watch how closely they have to dance together and sing their duets, I actually feel lucky that I didn't get the role.

Gladys isn't too bad a part. I get to sing a lot, and the "Steam Heat" and "Hernando's Hideaway" numbers are great fun, even if I have to dance with Sam Dolan. It's so obvious he's never danced before, and poor Miss Kerrigan might have a nervous breakdown before it's all over.

I'm also looking forward to the summer. I find out at the end of the month if I'm accepted into the writing program at Penn that I applied to. It seems like the perfect program for me, but it's awfully competitive. All I can do now is cross my fingers and hope for the best.

Oh my goodness, I almost forgot. I can't wait for the Valentine's Day dance.

13

Valentine's Day

CHOLLIE

I know it sounds hard to believe, but I think Billy's more excited than I am about the dance. He gives me all kinds of great advice as I get dressed.

Here are Billy Muller's Steps to Success.

Step 1: Keep an eye on Miranda at all times. But don't smother her, and make sure she doesn't see I'm watching her.

Step 2: Get out on the dance floor. Chicks love dancers.

Step 3: Request "Stairway to Heaven" from the DJ. When the DJ plays my song, I ask Miranda to dance.

Step 4: Always smile and look like I'm having a good time. But don't smile too much, or she'll think I'm crazy.

Step 5: Be sure to dance the last dance with Miranda. Apparently, a girl will always fall in love with whoever the lucky guy is she's dancing with at the end.

When we drive up to school, he starts going over the steps all over again, which is pretty helpful. Boy, the university lost a good guy when they tossed out Billy.

"Remember," Billy says as we pull up to the school, "you request 'Stairway to Heaven' by Led Zeppelin. Got it?"

"'Stairway to Heaven' by Led Zeppelin," I repeat.

Billy looks at me and smiles, then he takes a little bottle of cologne from the glove compartment and rubs some on my cheeks.

I hop out of the car but Billy calls me back and gives me some breath mints. He thinks of everything.

As I'm walking up to the school I'm feeling really good about myself. The basketball game feels far in the past. In fact, the school newspaper had a great article about the game today and I wasn't even blamed for the loss. And the whole thing with the student council and the toilet paper doesn't bother me at all anymore. In fact, I think it's kind of funny, and that puts a big smile on my face when I walk into the school.

The first person I see is Duke Samagura. I thank him and shake his hand because he was the one who wrote the really nice article in the school newspaper that didn't blame me for the loss. What a good guy.

Then I go right to the gym. It's really kind of cool, being in school at night and seeing everyone dressed a little nicer. And it's sort of mysterious going down the steps into the gym because there are balloons and streamers and red hearts, and you wouldn't even think you were going into the gym except for the smell that everyone's always complaining about but that I kind of like.

Music's playing, and it's so dark I'm afraid I'll trip over someone. No one's dancing yet and when I look across the dance floor, I see the light from the other side of the gym. The gym is split in half like last year. I look over on the other side and they need a fifth guy for the next game, and I figure this would be a great way for me to blow off some steam and not bother Miranda Mullaly too much.

Well, as I've already said, I'm a pretty good basketball player, and of course my team, with the help of Bobby Klotz crashing the boards and Colin Cromwell playing the point, has the floor for quite some time. In fact, I can't believe it when I look up at the clock in the gym and it's almost over. I miss the whole dance, if that's possible. I feel like one of those guys who accidentally travels through time.

I can't let my teammates down, so I keep playing until finally our game ends on a putback by Klotz. I shake hands really quick, and then I rush off to the other side of the gym and look for Miranda Mullaly. I'm nervous about going up to her and asking her to dance, but I'm really ready to do it.

I look around and I look around and I look around, but I don't see Miranda Mullaly. There are about twenty couples on the dance floor and I do my best to see if Miranda's out there with someone, but I don't see her. I rush up to the cafeteria and she's not there, either. So I run around the gym and I can't believe it. Miranda Mullaly is nowhere to be found.

What'll I say to Billy?

SAM

I have to shave quickly because Maureen and Sharon are banging on the door so Maureen can do Sharon's hair (what does that even mean?) for the dance. I get a nasty cut under my bottom lip as I scream at them to hold their horses. The Band-Aid stops the bleeding but it looks pretty bad, sort of like I've been punched in the lip. I guess I can always say, "You should see the other guy," if anyone asks.

As I check on the lip, blood drips on my only nice shirt, and then I can't find any deodorant. Everything we have smells like roses or cucumbers or melons. (Of course Dad doesn't care because he just uses what Mom buys.)

I leave the bathroom and go back into my room to change my shirt. Like I said, I don't own anything else this nice, so I have no other choice but to wear a Target sweater with blue and green stripes that I wear to school almost every day. I give myself a good look in the mirror. The cut lip and Band-Aid actually make me look sort of tough. I hope Miranda doesn't mind.

"Ready for the big dance, loverboy?"

I turn to see Maureen's on-again-off-again boyfriend, John Lutz, standing in my doorway. It's just my luck that Lutz (who my dad calls Putz) got his driver's license this week. It must be the easiest test in the world, because John Lutz is so dumb he couldn't spell "cat" if you gave him a C and an A and a T. Anyway, since my parents are having a special Valentine's date night (yuck!), I have to accept a ride to the dance with my two sisters and this moron Lutz.

We finally leave for the dance, and the whole time as he's driving Lutz looks in the rearview mirror and asks me who I'm going to be "sucking face" with. What does Maureen see in this guy? Anyway, I'm so nervous about dancing with Miranda that I don't reply to Lutz, even though I'm thinking of saying, "Your mom." And also, to tell the truth, Lutz makes me a little nervous. He's the epitome of a guy who would say, "Watch this!" and then crash his car into a wall or something.

The longest car ride ever finally comes to an end and I get to the dance. The first person I see at the dance is Duke Samagura, who's doing the check-in. Duke glares at me like he always does. He's probably still upset about the thumbtack that he *didn't* sit on. But I don't have time to talk to him or even glare back because I'm a man on a mission. I can't be bothered to tell Duke that he looks like an eighty-year-old nerd in his bow tie. I'm too busy looking for Miranda Mullaly.

After I check in, I go right to the gym and start looking around for Miranda. I don't see her anywhere, so I take up a post near the door that leads from the lobby so there's no way I'll miss her.

I'm just standing there waiting for her, all alone and honestly pretty bored. And I'm not the only one. Only a few people are dancing, and even though it's dark and there are decorations, you can tell it's the gym and you can *smell* the sweat and snot and dirty socks.

Some more people hit the dance floor, and I see Sharon out there. The girl loves to dance. And Ralph Waldo is right there with her, dancing like he's never danced before. But I don't see Miranda and sort of stay on the sidelines looking cool, though you can't look anything but bad when you're on the side of the dance floor and you're not talking to anyone. I look around but it's pretty dark. I can only see Erica Dickerson yakking away with some of her buddies and Mr. and Mrs. Porter quite possibly making out as they slow dance.

Some of the boys are on the other side, but I'm really not in the mood to give out wet willies or make fart sounds. There's been talk that they have some stink bombs that they're planning to set off. I really don't care.

Foxxy is out on the dance floor. He and Holly are dancing real slow to a fast song and I have to say it looks pretty cool. But seeing the two of them makes me feel alone, and I wonder if everyone is staring at me.

I don't have any choice but to leave the gym and do my best to look like I have something important to do. There's really nowhere to go but the bathroom, so that's where I go.

I don't know what's wrong with me. It's kind of weird, because I feel like crying. But I don't cry, which is good because if my eyes were red, somebody would think a girl dumped me or something like that, and then people would start talking and there would be about a thousand stories about me going around.

And I can't help but feel like I look stupid in the same old sweater I wear all the time, when everyone else is dressed up. And I can't help but think I smell like a girl, since I'm wearing lady deodorant. I actually start thinking of a plan to escape the dance. I mean, I really don't want to be here.

I get at least a good five minutes alone in the bathroom before someone else comes in.

"What are you doing in here?" Lichtensteiner asks me. He searches around, no doubt looking for toilet paper.

Believe it or not, Lichtensteiner suddenly makes me feel a lot better. "I'll let you guess, Mr. Lichtensteiner," I say, smiling for the first time all night.

Mr. Lichtensteiner huffs and puffs like the Big Bad Wolf. He takes a big breath of air through his nostrils, which is pretty disgusting, if you know what it smells like in the bathroom across from the cafeteria. Then he *smiles*. Like I always say, this is a sick man.

"And what happened to your lip?" Lichtensteiner asks.

I really want to tell him the truth, especially since I notice Lichtensteiner has trimmed his nose hairs.

"You should see the other guy," I say.

Just for a second I think I see a hint of a smirk on Lichtensteiner's face, like he gets the joke. Like he likes the joke. Then he sits on a sink like we're old buddies.

"So who's the lucky girl tonight, Dolan?"

"Huh?"

"Who's the lucky girl who gets to dance with Sam Dolan?" Lichtensteiner asks.

Suddenly I get the urge to tell him. Is that crazy?

But for the first time, I can't answer one of Lichtensteiner's questions. I mean, I'm really losing it. I just stand there like an idiot.

"Let me give you some advice, Dolan. You're not going to get a dance and a peck on the cheek in here," he says, gesturing toward the urinals.

"You're right," I say as I turn to leave, almost thanking him for getting me into a better mood.

I really don't want to watch Foxxy and everyone else having a good time in the gym, so I head into the cafeteria.

I get a warm soda (of course there's no ice) and a slice of cold pizza.

There I am, minding my own business, wishing the pizza was better and thinking of what to say to Miranda when I finally see her and ask her for a dance, when I hear somebody behind me.

"Ugh, can you close your mouth when you chew."

And this is not a question but more of a demand. And it's coming from Erica Dickerson. She's everywhere you don't want her to be, she really is.

I can't think of anything to say to her, so I keep gnawing on my pizza.

"Why don't you close your mouth and chew like a normal human being?"

What can you say when someone says that to you?

"That's not a very nice thing to say," I tell her, and I mean it, I really do. It sounds lame, of course, but it really isn't a nice thing to say.

"And you shouldn't put on a Band-Aid until you've stopped bleeding, Dolan," she says.

I wipe some of the blood off my chin with a napkin.

"I can take care of myself, thank you," I say, thinking I probably sound like Mary Poppins. But when Erica's around, everything I say sounds dumb.

"You should try pulling up your zipper, too. But don't worry, you won't have to be on your best behavior, because Miranda isn't here."

And then of course it hits me: I should've asked Miranda if she was going to the dance.

Duke

Neal and Cassandra have been pestering me all year to do something special for my birthday. I finally relented and allowed them to take me out to dinner before the Valentine's Day dance. We actually had a jolly good time. Neal and Cassandra were not overbearing and, to my great shock, did not give the waiter the third degree about the animals and vegetables we were about to eat.

After we were served our coffees and tea and chocolate mousse, Neal and Cassandra handed me a gift. It was a flat rectangular box tied with a blue bow. I graciously thanked them but couldn't help but think Cassandra had Googled: "What to give a precocious fourteen-year-old."

As soon as I opened the box, I felt like a big fat jerk. I was speechless as I looked down to see a gorgeous crimson-and-white-striped[22] bow tie.

My voice was filled with emotion as I thanked them. "It's simply, it's just absolutely . . . it's perfect."

Neal and Cassandra held hands and smiled at me. They were, *we* were, truly happy.

"Shall I wear it tonight?" I asked.

....
22. Harvard's colors!

"Of course," they replied in unison.

I wiped my hands on my napkin, untied the bow tie I was wearing, and carefully tied the birthday bow tie. All without looking in the mirror or watching a YouTube video. Even the waiter was impressed.

As we sipped our coffees and ate dessert, Cassandra beamed at me. "You look so handsome," she said. "Our little boy is growing up."

I shook my head and looked down at my coffee.

"So," Cassandra continued, sipping her coffee, "which lucky girl will be your dancing partner tonight?"

The intoxicating beauty of the bow tie and the thought that soon I'd be dancing with Miranda had the effect of eroding my defenses.

"Once I'm finished with my student council duties, then I'll have a dance, time permitting, with Miranda Mullaly."

I couldn't believe I had said it and felt myself blushing. Before they could pursue a line of questioning about Miranda, I quickly changed the subject to international affairs.

We were all in high spirits when Neal and Cassandra dropped me off at the dance. Cassandra even gave me a kiss and Neal shook my hand after I jumped out of the car. For the first time in a long while, I felt elated. Even though I'd be working the check-in alone with Mr. Porter and his wife, Polly, just knowing I'd be dancing with Miranda before the night was through made it all worthwhile.

I happily whistled a romantic tune as I entered the school, imagining Miranda's certain surprise earlier that day when she opened the candy-gram I had sent her. I felt very confident about the note I had attached to the heart-shaped lollipop:

She was a Phantom of delight
When first she gleam'd upon my sight;
A lovely Apparition, sent
To be a moment's ornament.[23]
Looking forward to seeing you at the dance.

Before she resigned from the student council, Miranda, the *wunderkind*,[24] had organized everything down to the last detail. So the only thing I had to do was shake hands with Mr. Porter and his wife, check in the student body, and wait to see Miranda.

"I've heard a lot about you," Polly said as I sat down beside her.

"Oh, that's nice," I said, pretending to read the list of

....

23. The first four lines of William Wordsworth's lovely "She Was a Phantom of Delight."

24. A person of remarkable talent who achieves great success at an early age.

students who had bought tickets. I had no desire to engage in any inane conversation.

"Oh, yes, Barry, or should I say Mr. Porter, ha-ha, is very impressed with your work on the student council. Of course, who wouldn't be impressed with an eighth-grader who carries a briefcase?"

Part of me wanted to tell Mrs. Polly Porter that I carry a briefcase because I take my education seriously. And I carry a briefcase in a feeble attempt to bring up the standards at Penn Valley. But I opted to daydream about my dance with Miranda instead of indulging Polly.

"And I adore your bow tie!"

At this point I would have simply excused myself, but I did not want to miss Miranda's entrance. Fortunately for me, students began to arrive, so Polly had something to do besides ask me questions and comment on my life.

I got right to work, happy to let the time pass as I checked in the students. And I noticed that some snow was beginning to fall outside. This was perfect, for I hoped to go to Miranda's house first thing in the morning if it snowed to help her father shovel his walk. What more could a girl ask for in a boyfriend?

Sam Dolan, the dolt, signed in with me. Sharon was with him, and she was good enough to ask if she could assist me. Obviously, all the manners (and talent) had skipped right past Sam and settled into Sharon. As Polly tried to find where the letter D could possibly be, I politely chatted with Sharon about the musical and she very kindly complimented my new bow tie.

I gave Sam the once-over. But I didn't have time for Sam and even waved off Knuckles and Moose, allowing him to go into the gym unmolested. I didn't even ask him why he was wearing a big Band-Aid on his face.

Moments later Chollie Muller entered the lobby, smiling like a madman.

"Hey, Duke, thanks for the nice article in the school newspaper. I felt really bad about the game until I read that. It cheered me up."

Just the thought of Ralph Waldo rewriting my newspaper article raised my blood pressure. If it weren't for the necessity of extracurricular activities to build up my transcript, I would've resigned from my position as sports editor.

Chollie left and, as if on cue, Ralph Waldo appeared. He wanted to talk about *The Pajama Game* and the school newspaper and was extremely curious to know whether Sharon Dolan had arrived. I couldn't take any more, so I smiled, closed my eyes, and watched as Knuckles and Moose returned to straighten out Ralph Waldo. He would not destroy another article of mine ever again.

After that, things quieted down in the lobby. Mr. and Mrs. Porter finally left me alone and went into the gym. I listened to the music, tapped my foot, and waited.

And I waited.

And I waited.

But there was no Miranda Mullaly.

Soon students began to leave the dance. And I was still at the check-in desk, waiting for Miranda. I felt silly and embarrassed, sitting there all alone. I put my hand up to my bow tie and was overcome by the feeling that I looked foolish. I took off the bow tie and stuffed it in my pocket.

Just then, Sharon Dolan appeared. She began to talk about the musical, but I couldn't understand what she was saying. I stared at her, thinking of Miranda Mullaly.

I blinked my eyes. "Huh?"

I had more important things on my mind than *The Pajama Game*. Sharon wished me a happy Valentine's Day, gave me a heart-shaped lollipop, and went on her way.

I was alone again. Looking at the lollipop Sharon left me, I suddenly wondered if I had signed Miranda's candygram. I could not, for the life of me, recall if I had signed it or not. And then I was *certain* I forgot to sign the candygram, so Miranda would not have understood the note and without a signature probably would have dropped it in the trash.

And then, suddenly, the dance was over.

And then, suddenly, Neal and Cassandra were driving me home.

"Duke, did you hear me?" Cassandra asked.

"Huh?" was the only reply I could muster.

"Did you have a good time at the dance, dear?"

"It was okay."

"What happened to your tie?"

"Oh, it's in my pocket. It became a little loose, so I had to take it off."

Neal nodded and we were silent.

I had to pinch myself. How did I go from waiting for Miranda at the dance to sitting in the backseat of my parents' car? Where had the time gone? And, most importantly, where was Miranda Mullaly?

"Did you get to dance with your special friend?"

I didn't answer and closed my eyes. What began as a dream had become a nightmare.

Miranda

To: Tom

From: Miranda

Date: February 12, 2016 10:55 PM

Subject: Thank you for the greatest night of my life!

Tom,

I can't sleep. My thoughts are still of tonight and our time together. How perfect were the snowflakes falling from the sky when the dance ended? The night was truly wonderful. It was magical. It was a miracle.

I was honored to be on your arm and to meet your friends and to see your school. It's hard to believe our schools neighbor each other. They are so different.

Thank you very much for saving me from the Penn Valley dance where I'm sure they were throwing toilet paper and pizza at one another. I can't believe how clean your school is. Penn Valley is dirty and our gym smells. I feel like a princess who has been saved from heathens. Though, I do feel bad about leaving Erica to fend for herself . . .

Last but not least, I forgot to thank you for the surprise candy-gram. How did you purchase a candy-gram at my school? I had no idea you had a poetic side. It was so romantic!

I've been thinking a lot about what you said about your graduation dance in June. I think it would be marvelous to rent a limo, but if you can't afford it my father has already volunteered to drive us in his new car. Oh, I can't wait!

Will the snow ever melt?

Will the flowers ever grow again?

Will I ever be in your arms again?

Big big happy sad (only because I miss you) hugs!

Always yours,

Miranda

14

The Snow Day

SAM

Miranda Mullaly's father is a hairy man who runs very fast.

And he has a bad temper. Not the kind of guy who likes to joke around, I think.

Let me start at the beginning.

I wake up this morning to the sound of a shovel scraping the pavement. I'm in big trouble if Dad's out shoveling, so I jump out of bed. But when I look out the window, who do I see? John Lutz.

I'm looking at the snow and this weird feeling comes over me. I think about how much fun it will be to go sledding and have a snowball fight, and I feel just like a little kid. And then I remember how rotten I felt about the dance and how I was all alone and how the only real conversations I had were with Lichtensteiner and Erica Dickerson. What's wrong with me?

But then the good feeling about the snow makes me feel better about the bad feeling about the dance and I get dressed and get on with the day. I decide to go out and help (if Mom and Dad wake up, they'll make me go out and shovel anyway).

Outside, it's cold and bright and windy. But the air feels good in my lungs.

"You know, my father won't pay you for this," I tell Lutz.

Lutz stops and looks at me.

"That ain't why I'm shoveling the walk, dummy," he says, and continues to heave huge shovelfuls of snow in a pile.

"Then why are you doing it?" I ask.

Lutz stops, leans against his shovel, and looks at me like I'm an idiot.

"Are you an idiot?" he asks.

"No."

"I'm shoveling because your sister's mad at me."

"So? My sister doesn't have to shovel the walk. My dad's the one who will be happy."

Lutz shakes his head and continues shoveling.

"If you knew anything about girls, Sam, you'd know that when you do something helpful and useful and kind, like shoveling a sidewalk and driveway, you get on their good side."

I don't say a word, but I shovel and help Lutz finish. He's some kind of snow shoveler, and we're done in less than five minutes. Then I hear the door open and Maureen's voice.

"John? Is that you?"

Lutz bows.

"Oh, John, thank you so much. Come inside. You must be freezing."

You would've thought Lutz cured cancer or something, the way Mom and Maureen dote on him. They give him hot chocolate and pieces of toast, and Mom is cooking bacon and scrambling eggs. Lutz looks at me and winks.

And then it hits me. Lutz is right. I *am* an idiot.

I jump up out of my seat and run to Miranda Mullaly's house.

As I'm running I can't help thinking that Lutz is no fool. In fact, Lutz saves the day because I'm sure Miranda will invite me inside for hot chocolate and to meet her parents, and she'll probably say, "This is the boy from school I was telling you about."

So when I get to Miranda's house, I have a big smile on

my face and I am ready to go. I mean, I have enough energy to dig out the Panama Canal.

So you can imagine my disappointment when I arrive and I see Chollie Muller already digging the snow. Chollie is on the sidewalk, shoveling away like he's been doing it his whole life. And if you drove by, you would've thought Chollie lived there. But of course I know better because I've seen Chollie at the basketball game and I've watched him with Miranda in the library. So I know Chollie's very, very interested in Miranda. And now that I'm here, I bet he's figured out that I'm very, very interested in Miranda also.

So I start right in. Like I said, I have enough energy to shovel the whole town. I feel like I can move mountains of snow.

Chollie's on one end and I'm on the other and it's a pretty big sidewalk. We race to the middle and we meet in no time. We both stop and look up at the house. The front door is right in the center, so we start clearing out the walkway and I can't wait to get to the door because I'm just figuring Miranda will be there and I can't wait to see her. And I just *have* to be the first one to see her.

Chollie and I stop at the front door and I look back at the street and I can't believe what I see. Across the street, Duke Samagura is shoveling out a car.

I look back at the house we just shoveled out. Written

there on the mailbox in really big letters is MINKIN. And then the door opens, and it's Mr. Minkin, my English teacher.

"Good morning, gentlemen," he says, just as if we were walking into his classroom. "I must thank you for shoveling my walk. . . ."

I don't listen to anything else he says because now I know Miranda Mullaly lives in the house across the street. Where Duke Samagura is shoveling snow.

I dash across the street and start shoveling, but it all goes downhill from there.

Miranda

To: Erica

From: Miranda

Date: February 13, 2016 8:46 AM

Subject: Call me!!!

_____

E,

Call me when you get this! Please! Tom broke up with me . . .

M

CHOLLIE

Billy wakes me early in the morning.

"Let's go, big fella," he says. "It's snowing."

"You wanna go sledding?" I ask.

"No, Chollie, I'm tired." He yawns and sort of looks like he's been up all night. "I'm just giving you some advice."

I jump out of bed and look out the window. There sure is a lot of snow out there.

"What's the advice?"

Billy stretches and yawns some more and says, "You've got to go out there and shovel your little lady friend's walk."

"You think so?"

"Absolutely. You'll get in good with her old man, and girls love that."

I hop right to it, getting dressed as fast as I can, thinking the whole time how lucky I am to have a big brother like Billy who knows everything.

Miranda's house is only a couple of blocks away. The world is so quiet this early in the morning and the only sound seems to be the snow crunching under my boots. It's really nice. And I can't help but think the only thing to make it better would be walking along with Miranda. But it is all okay because I'll probably be seeing her soon enough.

In fact, I'm pretty certain she'll invite me in for pancakes and bacon.

But then I get all worried about why she wasn't at the dance. I hope she's okay and it wasn't anything bad, like her mom or dad getting sick or maybe her pet dying. There are lots of possible reasons, but I can't figure any of them out. And more than anything, I'm glad Billy wasn't there when I got home last night because I didn't want to disappoint him after he did so much work to get me ready for the dance.

When I get to her house, I start with the sidewalk. But before I even get a chance to really start digging, I see Sam Dolan. What's he doing here? I get pretty competitive and we both start digging and shoveling. In seconds we're right smack in the middle of the sidewalk in front of the house. I wait for Sam to say something. He always has something snarky to say. But instead he just starts shoveling up the walkway to the house. And I'm right there with him.

I'm really confused about what Sam is doing here. Unless, of course, he's in love with Miranda, too. Billy always says there's going to be competition for a great girl like Miranda. I'm just about to ask him what's up when Mr. Minkin comes out of the house, and we realize we've been shoveling the wrong walk. That's when I see Duke in the driveway across the street, digging out someone else's car, and Sam and I must have the same thought. We leave Mr. Minkin at his door, scratching his head.

As we race across the street, I see the mailbox that, sure enough, says MULLALY, so I feel good about everything now. At least I know I'm not wasting my time. Sam and I start shoveling her sidewalk.

When we meet in the middle, Duke marches up to us from behind the car. Then he starts messing up all the work we did, but I don't care. I really don't. I'm just going to clear the walkway up to the front door and then ring the doorbell and introduce myself to Mr. Mullaly. I really am. I'm not going to miss free throws anymore. I'm not going to fumble footballs anymore. I'm not going to be afraid to ask Miranda to dances anymore.

To: Erica

From: Miranda

Date: February 13, 2016 9:02 AM

Subject: Call me!!!

E

I called him, and do you know what he said? He said, "Why are you calling?" And I didn't know what to say. And after I didn't say anything Tom said, "Miranda, it's over." And I wanted to ask why, why, why, why, why but I didn't.

Call me if you get a chance.

M

Duke

The worst invention in the history of the world must be the snooze button. Thanks to this scourge against humanity, I woke up late and had to scramble to get to Miranda Mullaly's house so I could shovel her walk. I looked sadly at my bow tie one last time, then closed my bedroom door and left for Miranda's house on 1615 Cherry Lane.

I still had a bitter taste in my mouth because of the disaster at the dance, but I felt alive again walking through the winter wonderland. The scene reminded me of the poem "Snow flakes" by Emily Dickinson that Mr. Minkin had *unsuccessfully* tried to teach us.

> *I counted till they danced so*
> *Their slippers leaped the town—*
> *And then I took a pencil*
> *To note the rebels down—*
> *And then they grew so jolly*
> *I did resign the prig—*
> *And ten of my once stately toes*
> *Are marshalled for a jig!*

Just to help you understand how high my spirits were,

I was thinking on the stroll over how Mr. Mullaly would be so impressed by my work ethic he would invite me in for cocoa or a warm cider. My conversation would, of course, be so mature and erudite[25] Mr. Mullaly would probably offer me a job at his law firm, though I don't know for sure if he's a lawyer. Sadly, I would have to tell him my plans for Harvard, and then of course I would offer to keep an eye on Miranda while we were students together.

So despite the disaster of the dance, I felt pretty good about my prospects as I approached the Mullaly house armed with my shovel.

And then I stopped, shocked—no, absolutely stupefied—at what I saw happening across the street from the Mullaly house. There, shoveling like men possessed, were Chollie and Sam. I walked quietly through the snow and up the Mullaly driveway so the two imbeciles wouldn't be able to see me. Then, behind the car, I quietly began to shovel out the driveway.

When I looked up to check on my nemeses, they saw me and ran across the street. Sadly, because of the snow, no cars were able to run them over. With the eagerness of puppies they began to shovel the sidewalk and got a fair amount done. In fact, I almost thought they were

....
25. Learned; well educated.

working together to foil my impeccable plan.

When I had the car properly dug out, I decided to have a word with the two bozos. I approached them, my shovel on my shoulder like a long rifle.[26]

"What are you two doing here?" I asked them.

They continued to shovel and were now clearing the walkway to the front door. I had no choice at this point but to go over to the sidewalk and cover it with the snow they had already cleared. And that's exactly what I did. When Sam saw what I was doing, he went over to the car and began to cover up what I had moments earlier so expertly cleared. Chollie continued to shovel up the walkway to the front door.

In order to stop Sam from destroying my hard work, I nailed him in the ear with a snowball. Sam is so dumb he couldn't think of anything else but to return a snowball my way. I easily ducked to avoid the onslaught but Sam continued to pepper snowballs in my direction. Then suddenly I saw something out of the corner of my eye. Could it be Miranda looking out her bedroom window? At that same moment, Sam finally hit his mark and got me square in the face.

I slowly wiped the snow from my left eye and walked

....

26. The fairly inaccurate rifle commonly used during the colonial period and the American Revolution.

with purpose toward Sam to whack him in the head with my shovel. It was something I should have done a long time ago. It was something I should have done when he put the thumbtack on my seat.

As I approached, Sam was preparing to nail Chollie with a snowball to keep him from clearing the walkway to the house. I let loose with the shovel to clobber Sam the moment he threw his snowball at Chollie. I was going to let Sam have it for not only the snowball and thumbtack but for making fun of my briefcase and, yes, for the way he *looked* at my bow tie last night.

Alas, I was undone by my desire for revenge against Sam. I swung the shovel so hard I slipped, missing Sam and smashing the passenger window of Mr. Mullaly's Mercedes-Benz. The impact set off the car alarm, which I can attest works very well.

The only saving grace was Sam's snowball. It missed Chollie, who ducked right in time, and scored a direct hit into Mr. Mullaly's face the moment he opened his front door. Mr. Mullaly, a hirsute[27] and ugly beast, stumbled and wailed, waving his great arms and falling back into the house and flat on his derrière.

On my back, I was momentarily stunned. But there

....
27. Covered with hair; hairy.

was little time to collect my thoughts before Mr. Mullaly regained his footing and jumped out the front door again. The scene was chaotic, what with the car alarm blaring and Chollie and Sam screaming.

Mr. Mullaly slipped and fell once again, raging and bellowing and screaming, "My back! My new car! My back!"

I ran and ran and ran, not stopping until I reached the warmth of my house.

As there was no report of a massacre on Cherry Lane on the evening news, I can only sadly surmise that Mr. Mullaly did not catch up with Sam and Chollie.

Miranda

To: Erica

From: Miranda

Date: February 13, 2016 9:13 AM

Subject: Thanks

E,

You'll never guess what happened after we hung up (thanks for being there, by the way!). Chollie, Duke, and Sam were shoveling our walk and then started fighting. They attacked my father with a barrage of snowballs and smashed the window of my dad's new car.

My dad flipped out and hurt his back chasing them. I'm so embarrassed.

This house is crazy. Can you come over? You just have to see it.

M ☺ ☹

15

The Worst Weekend in the History of Bad Weekends

SAM

I've had a lot of bad weekends, but this is the worst weekend in the history of bad weekends. It's without a doubt the worst weekend since last Halloween, when Foxxy and I got nailed throwing toilet paper into the trees outside of the school. Why Lichtensteiner was at school that night, I'll never know. And this is much worse than the weekend I was punished for starting a teeny-weeny little fire in the science lab. And even worse than the weekend I was punished after using the school intercom to find out if anyone had seen my missing winter gloves.

This weekend is the worst because I haven't been *caught* yet.

After narrowly escaping the clutches of Mr. Mullaly, I am on edge. I mean, really on edge. My heart skips a beat and I jump every time a phone rings. And then when I forget for just a moment about the snow-shoveling disaster, I remember that Miranda wasn't at the dance, and that hurts, too.

To make matters worse, John Lutz is still hanging around the house. When I go into the kitchen to make a sandwich, he's there. When I go into the den to watch some television, he's there, too. And he's got his dirty hand wrapped around the remote control. I swear Lutz is like a female Erica Dickerson. He's everywhere you don't want him to be.

I'm about to tell him to stop changing the channel when the phone rings.

"Sam," Mom calls from the kitchen, "it's for you."

I freeze in my seat and suddenly begin to sweat. And I'm really thirsty. It must be Mr. Mullaly calling to tell me he's going to beat the stuffing out of me because of the snowball.

"Go on, get the phone, moron," Lutz says.

I still can't move, and that's saying something because I hate being in the same room as Lutz. Then Mom comes into the room and she's talking on the phone.

"Okay, and best to your mom," she says before tossing it to me.

"Hello . . ." I say.

"Sam, Foxxy here."

For the first time since forever, or I suppose since an hour or two, I feel alive again.

"Foxxy! Foxxy!" I turn and look at Lutz and point to the phone. "It's Foxxy," I tell Lutz. I just have to share my relief with somebody.

"Foxxy, what's happening?" I ask.

"You up for some sledding?"

"You bet," I say. It's just what I need. I need to talk to Foxxy and tell him what's happening. If anyone can help me out of this mess and make me feel better, it's Foxxy.

"Great, Holly and I are heading over to the golf course. I heard the sledding is awesome. Do you want us to stop by on the way over?"

"No, no," I say. "I'll meet you there."

"Hey, you okay?" Foxxy asks.

"I'm fine. Did you have fun last night?"

"It was great. Holly and I had the best time."

"Great," I say. "I'll see you for sledding later on, okay?"

But I have no intention of sledding with Foxxy *and* Holly Culver. I saw enough of them last night. And believe me, they wouldn't be talking to old Sam Dolan while we were sledding. I feel bad enough without being a third wheel.

So I spend the rest of the day in my room. It's one of these days where I just can't stand any other human beings.

When I finally emerge, everyone is cuddled up in the

living room. And Lutz is acting like he's a part of the family. Sharon, Maureen, Mom, and Dad have hot chocolates and they're sharing the covers. And Lutz is sitting right in the middle, where I should be sitting.

I'm standing, looking at them all cuddling together, happy as can be. And there isn't room for me.

"What about date night?" I ask. The girls and Mom are supposed to go out and me and Dad are supposed to stay home and eat pizza and watch movies. John Lutz is *not* supposed to be part of any of this.

"We've decided to stay in tonight," Mom says. "It's too cold."

Mentioning the cold is the signal for Maureen to cuddle with Lutz. This is enough to turn my stomach.

Mom is the only one who notices me.

"Do you feel okay, honey?" she asks.

I shrug.

Mom puts her hot chocolate down and gets up from under the covers. She puts her hand on my forehead and I can feel her warmth.

"You don't look well. Do you want to rest in bed?"

Suddenly I feel like hugging Mom and crying and really telling her about everything that has happened. I mean, I have a lot of emotions going on inside of me. Thankfully, I don't cry (Lutz would never let me live it

down) and Mom just thinks I'm coming down with something.

Before I know it, I'm tucked under my warm covers
and I have the second Twilight book to read. Mom gives
me a kiss and leaves, and for the first time, I feel all right. I
think it's going to be okay.

In no time I'm asleep, but it's like the old movie *A Nightmare on Elm Street.* The difference is it's not Freddy Krueger
who's after me, it's Mr. Mullaly. And this time, I'm the one
wearing underwear and he's chasing me through the hall-
ways of Penn Valley, and Lichtensteiner and the boys are
laughing. And Miranda watches, horrified.

I wake up screaming. Once I realize I'm safe, I hop out
of bed and write out a list.

How to make this up to Miranda Mullaly so she'll be
my girlfriend:

* _____

* _____

* _____

* _____

All I can come up with is blanks.

Maybe Erica Dickerson is right. Maybe I am an idiot.

CHOLLIE

For some reason Billy thinks everything that happened at the Mullaly house is hilarious. But I'm honestly having a hard time laughing about it. And it really hurts that Billy of all people is laughing at me.

"Tell me again," he says, wiping tears from his eyes.

"Come on, Billy, I told you like ten times already."

Just telling the story is frightening. I have never seen the look that Mr. Mullaly had in his eyes on another human being before. I don't know what he would've done to me if he hadn't slipped on that ice.

"Just tell me exactly what happened with the broken window and the snowball," he says, and he closes his eyes and rubs his head like a fortune-teller. "I need to see clearly what happened so I can figure out where we go from here."

So I tell Billy the whole crazy, embarrassing story all over again. He stops me toward the end.

"What exactly did you see as you were walking up to the door?"

"I looked back and Sam was throwing a snowball at me. I ducked and it hit Mr. Mullaly right in the face. It was like a scene out of a movie, the way he fell back and screamed."

Billy still has his eyes closed but he's trying not to laugh. "Go on," he says.

"Duke swung the shovel and missed Sam and smashed the car window. The car alarm was really loud and Mr. Mullaly ran outside yelling and he slipped and I ran and ran and ran the whole way home."

Billy doesn't say anything for a minute and then opens his eyes and smiles. And it's his good smile, his helpful smile. Not his smile that says he's laughing at me.

"Hey, Chollie, you know what?"

"What?"

"You're in the clear on this thing. You didn't break the car window, did you?"

"No."

"And you didn't hit Mr. Mullaly in the face with a snow-ball, did you?"

"Yeah, that's right. All I did was shovel the walk."

"You're clean in this, Chollie. You're going to come out of this smelling like a rose."

Billy's right. I didn't do anything wrong. And for the first time since it all happened, I feel hungry. And I really feel like a weight has been lifted, like I can breathe again.

"So what should I do?" I ask, rubbing my hands together.

"It's obvious these other two dudes weren't shoveling

for their health. They were shoveling for the same reason you were. There's competition. So you need to forget about hoping to see her at a dance or anything like that. Now is the time to act."

"Should I call her right now and explain what happened?"

"I don't recommend that. Her father is probably still stewing about the broken window and the snowball in the face. I know I'd be pretty mad."

Billy takes his phone and starts working on it.

"I'll tell you what, Chollie. I'm going to free up Friday night and drive you and Miranda to the movies." He looks up at me. "So as soon as you see her at school, go up to her and ask her out. Friday night. Movie. You and Miranda Mullaly."

Duke

Never before has a young man looked forward to reading a sociological manuscript more than I did that afternoon. I usually dread reading Neal and Cassandra's academic work, but the manuscript (*Ethel's Story*, if you recall) was just what I needed to keep my mind from stewing over Sam and Chollie.

When I came to the midpoint of their study, I got up from my desk and stretched and made myself a cup of tea. I contemplated calling the Mullaly abode and explaining myself but thought maybe I'd wait a couple of days to allow Mr. Mullaly to calm down.

Mr. Mullaly is surprisingly foulmouthed, and I was shaken to the core as he bolted from his house. But who could blame him after Sam had pelted him with snowballs? My only regret is that Mr. Mullaly didn't catch Sam. And there is the little matter of my lightly tapping Mr. Mullaly's car. Blast Sam Dolan for ducking! I'm certain that when Mr. Mullaly meets me and sees the kind of fellow I am, there won't be any hard feelings. I can even tell him I was protecting him from Sam's unprovoked snowball attack.

Perhaps we'll even laugh about the whole thing.

Perhaps he won't even want my money for the broken

car window; though, being a gentleman, I'll certainly offer to pay for the damages.

Perhaps he will agree with me that Chollie and Sam were totally out of line. After all, I was at the Mullaly house first.

I finished the manuscript and tried to no avail to clear Sam and Chollie from my head. Marcus Aurelius[28] wrote long ago, "The true worth of a man is to be measured by the objects he pursues." Clearly, in this day and age, Miranda is not to be referred to as an "object" but as an erudite, passionate, and empowered young woman. And obviously my pursuit of Miranda says a lot about me, and about Miranda as well. But what I simply cannot comprehend is how Sam and Chollie—neither of whom could count past ten without the help of their toes—figure into the equation.

If they really think they are going to steal Miranda's heart from me, they are both sorely mistaken.

....

28. Joint sixteenth emperor of the Roman Empire. Especially remembered for his philosophical writings.

16

Can Things Get Any Worse?

SAM

Lichtensteiner, the jerk, is the first to say something. And just when I thought we were on better terms after our little powwow in the bathroom Friday night.

"Did you enjoy the snow this weekend?" he asks me after I get off the bus. I'm hardly in the school.

I stop and try to read his face as all the students pass us by.

"It was all right," I say, trying not to look at the blueberry muffin pieces trapped in his teeth. But there's no escaping his grossness. He's got a big smile on his face.

"Did you shovel some walks, Dolan?"

"I shoveled a couple of walks," I answer.

"That's great, Dolan. You know, I would ask you to shovel my sidewalk and driveway, but I just got a new car."

Lichtensteiner laughs and laughs and laughs. So much for burying the hatchet. I sort of run away from him and go to the cafeteria because the last person I want to see is Miranda Mullaly in biology class.

I feel a little bit better when I spot Foxxy and the boys messing around like they always do. It's sort of like family and I practically have tears in my eyes when I see them. But then as I walk over they're laughing and also making noises. As I get closer I hear they are making the sound of shattering glass with each step I take.

I stop and they stop. Then I take another step and again they all make the sound of shattering glass.

As I walk closer they pretend they're being hit by snowballs.

I stop again and this time when I stop, they begin to make kissing noises and I hear a couple of them singing, "Sam and Miranda sitting in a tree . . ." What are these guys, like, in the first grade? Grow up.

And even though Foxxy is there without Holly Culver for the first time since they've been going out, and I really need to talk to him, I leave the cafeteria. It's all just too embarrassing to stick around.

When Erica Dickerson sees me in science class, her

smile is even bigger than Lichtensteiner's. And during the lab, when we're supposed to be working, Erica tells me everything. Like how Mr. Mullaly wants to break my neck. Like how Miranda is really embarrassed because her father was running down the street in the snow half-naked.

And I have to listen to this even though I haven't gotten any sleep thanks to my nightmares.

I realize now that I'm the guy who should be in my book *Watch This!*

I really don't think it can get any worse.

Duke

Knuckles and Moose have had a very busy day.

Jimmy Foxx is the first to feel their wrath. He thought it would be funny to make the noise of breaking glass as I walked down the hallway.

I stopped and looked at Foxx.

"Are these sounds supposed to mean something?" I asked.

Foxx is a friend of Sam Dolan and these guys are all alike, with their lowbrow humor. He just nodded like an imbecile.

One of Foxx's confederates joined in.

"Hey, Duke, does Miranda Mullaly have a thing for guys in bow ties?"

I quickly clapped my hands twice, and Knuckles and Moose emerged from the shadows and took care of business.

It was once written, some say, by Winston Churchill,[29] "If you are going through hell, keep going." I don't know if he had any days like this, but it is sound advice. I went through the day quietly and did not respond to any of the jokes or jibes from my classmates. I let Knuckles and Moose do the

....
29. The great British prime minister and Nobel Prize winner.

talking. After lunch I took haven in Mr. Wexler's room. He was kind enough to excuse me from art class.

It got worse when I got home from rehearsals.

Cassandra and Neal could not hide their emotions. They both put their hands to their mouths when I walked through the door.

"Oh, Duke, Duke, Duke," Cassandra said as she walked toward me with her hands out. "What happened? Tell me, what happened?"

Neal stood and watched the scene. He only needed a pipe to look like some fantasy father from a fifties television program.[30]

"Tell us what happened, son."

"Mullaly?" I asked.

Neal nodded.

"He called today," Cassandra explained.

"What took him so long?" I asked. Maybe my voice was a little gruff, a little uncaring, a little bit the way Knuckles and Moose would sound if they talked. But I have changed. I'm not sure if it's from reading too much James Thurber[31] or simply from turning fourteen.

....

30. See the nauseating *Father Knows Best*.

31. The great American humorist. See especially "The Remarkable Case of Mr. Bruhl" and "The Secret Life of Walter Mitty."

Cassandra looked at me as if she were seeing me for the first time. "I think we need some tea. Let's sit down and talk this over, okay?"

She scampered off to the kitchen and Neal took her place, putting his hand on my shoulder. He looked down at me oddly. It was a look in his eyes I'd never seen before.

We stood quietly till Cassandra called us in for tea.

"I have your favorite, Earl Grey," she said as she poured me a cup. "Tell us, please, Duke, what happened?"

I don't know what came over me, but I didn't say a word. I only stared at her, and then began to nibble on my biscotto.

"Duke?" she prodded. "You can tell me."

What could I say? Could I tell her how I didn't have the guts to speak to Miranda? Could I tell her how I felt truly alone? Could I say I was now embarrassed to wear my bow tie? I said nothing.

"Duke, we want you to know that we are here for you," Neal said.

"Would you like to see Dr. Todd again?" Cassandra asked.

I had to laugh at that, especially since Knuckles and Moose were standing right behind them, eyeing the biscotti and cookies on the table.

"Now, don't misunderstand us," Neal said. "We're

thrilled that you were out playing with your friends. It's just that, well, from what Mr. Mullaly said, things got a little out of hand."

I looked Neal directly in his eyes, took my teacup, and finished my Earl Grey.

"We told Mr. Mullaly we would pay for the damage to his window," Cassandra added.

I nodded to Cassandra, held on to the edge of the table, and pushed out my chair. I silently marched out of the room without looking back.

When I got to my room, I did something I have never done before: I slammed the door like a petulant child. And it actually felt good.

Slamming doors is a great reliever of stress.

CHOLLIE

School is pretty weird today. Everyone knows about what happened at Miranda's house this weekend. So it's super uncomfortable working with Miranda during science. I go from getting ready to ask her if she's busy on Friday night to preparing myself to answer awkward questions about what happened.

But Miranda doesn't say anything. She just goes about her work and it's really, really terrible.

She doesn't smile like she usually does.

She doesn't ask me if I had a nice weekend, which she usually does.

She doesn't ask me if I would like to copy her notes, which she usually does.

And the day gets even worse when I come home and see Billy.

"We got a problem, kid," Billy says.

"What?" I say.

"Mr. Mullaly called."

17

The Play's the Thing

CHOLLIE

Even though Billy says I'm in the driver's seat, it sure doesn't feel that way. Miranda hasn't said a word to me all week, and I really can't ask her out because everything's different now. Not only does Miranda not talk but her smile is gone, too. She almost looks like she could burst into tears at any moment.

But even worse is what's happening at home. Ever since Mr. Mullaly called, my mom says Billy has been a bad influence on me and she's sick of him lying on the couch all day.

She brings up the subject over dinner.

Mom says, "Today, while you were lying on the couch all day wasting your life watching television and texting and whatever else you do, I called Uncle Tommy."

Billy says, "How's Uncle Tommy?"

Mom says, "Uncle Tommy is in need of a full-time pizza delivery boy. And you got the job."

"But that's an hour away."

Mom goes on eating and says, "You're going to move in with him."

Billy looks at my dad for help.

"You heard your mother," Dad says.

"I think Chollie needs an older brother to help him navigate the turbulent waters of middle school," Billy says as he ruffles my hair.

I think it's a really nice thing to say, but Mom and Dad laugh so hard they practically fall out of their seats.

"You're moving out, working for Uncle Tommy, and then reenrolling in college next semester," Mom says, biting a carrot.

And that's the end of the discussion, because when Mom says something, it's the law.

So now here I am, with Miranda not talking to me when we're in science class and me trying to figure out what I'm supposed to do in a play I only joined to get closer to her.

And here we are in Billy's room. It's Friday night and Billy is supposed to take me and Miranda to the movies, but instead Billy's packing up his stuff.

If that's being in the driver's seat, then it's being in the driver's seat right before a crash.

Duke

If it weren't for the play, I don't know how I would've survived the week. All week my classmates, for lack of a better word, made snide comments about my snow-shoveling abilities and my intentions where Miranda Mullaly is concerned. Poor Knuckles and Moose had to work overtime to keep the jokers in line. It was only the thought of getting up on the stage each afternoon that kept me going.

The rehearsals have been, surprisingly, moving along.

Besides Chollie Muller, who probably couldn't fart and chew gum at the same time,[32] our cast is talented. Sam Dolan has actually learned his lines. And even his sister Sharon, who will be spending a goodish amount of time with me on the stage, appears to be able to hold her own.

And then, of course, there's Miranda. I had forgotten how often her character, Gladys, is on stage with Sid. We have an amazing number together called "Hernando's Hideaway," which we will block and begin rehearsing next week.

This might be my last opportunity to sweep Miranda Mullaly off her feet.

....
32. This is what Lyndon Johnson once said about Gerald Ford.

SAM

So I'm sitting alone in my room. It's exactly seven o'clock. It's date night, and Dad is waiting downstairs, deciding on which movie to watch and waiting for the pizza to be delivered.

It's exactly one week since the debacle at the dance and I feel like I'm still dealing with the aftermath in every part of my life.

I feel rotten because Sharon is really upset with me. Usually when Sharon is mad and says I embarrass her, like the time Foxxy and I scared her friends when she had a slumber party, it lasts for only a day. But this time it's different. I can see how hard she's working on the play. After all, she's the star. She begged me with tears in her eyes not to mess up the play for her. I really wish she would've threatened and screamed at me like usual. Then I would've felt better. But now I feel embarrassed not only for myself but for Sharon, too. I think I'm finally going crazy.

Miranda isn't acting the same. I don't think she smiled once all week. More than anything, I want to call her and tell her how sorry I am about the car window and tell her how great she is in the play. But I can't. I have no idea how to say it. And I really don't think I could say anything, because she looks angry and I have this feeling it's because of me.

Erica Dickerson won't stop talking about the snow shoveling. She really wants me to tell her why I was there. And even though I think Erica's pretty dense, I know she's not *that* dense.

Mom is really upset about the snowball I hit Mr. Mullaly with. Of course, I'm the one who should be upset since I've been terrorized by nightmares ever since. All that hard work trying to be good and this is what happens.

John Lutz really came through, though. The night after Mr. Mullaly called, Lutz stayed (even though he wasn't invited) for dinner. He finished the last pork chop, which made Dad angry. Then he gave Mom his empty plate as if Mom were a waitress. I could tell she wanted to smash it over his head, but she didn't. That seemed to divert attention away from me.

Another distraction has been the play. There's more to my part than I thought. I'm one of the first people to go up on stage and speak after the big song to start off the show. My speech is called the exposition and I kind of tell the audience what's happening. (Chollie is with me and only has to say, "He don't belong in this town," but he can't really do it.)

Next week I'm going to start rehearsing a dance scene with Miranda. It's going to be me, Ralph Waldo (who's practically a professional dancer), and Miranda. I just know I'll be able to make it up to her with this dance.

Miranda

To: Erica

From: Miranda

Date: February 19, 2016 9:07 PM

Subject: Sorry

E,

I lied when I told you I couldn't go to the movies tonight. I wasn't grounded. You know what I'm doing? Sitting alone in my room and thinking about how a week ago I was at the dance with Tom and everything seemed right in the world. Then in one day, Tom dumps me by e-mail, and Chollie, Sam, and Duke decide to ruin my life, and my dad's new car, on a perfectly beautiful winter day.

I also have to apologize for not having lunch with you this week. I didn't have any work to do on the yearbook. I was actually hiding in the library. There was no way I could go to the cafeteria with all the teasing about Saturday.

Please don't think I've been avoiding you. I only meant to avoid everyone else. I just can't deal right now. Please forgive me.

M ☹

Freewriting

Sam Dolan
February 29th
English 8A
Mr. Minkin

Suggested Writing Prompt: *Think about something or someone that annoys or bothers you. Write about what it is and why it bothers you. What can you do to make it less irritating?*

Hey Mr. Minkin,

This is the easiest question ever in the history of writing prompts. I'm up to my ears in Erica Dickerson, I really am. She is the most annoying and bothersome girl in the school, in the town, in the state, in the country, on the planet, in the solar system, and in the expanding universe.

Why does she bother me?

There are so many reasons. First, she is my science lab partner and acts like we're good buddies when we're not. And then she's pals with Miranda Mullaly and it seems that every time I have a chance to talk to Miranda, Erica is with her. It's like she's Miranda's bodyguard or something. What I can't understand is why a smart, classy girl like Miranda is friends with someone as uncouth (thanks for the vocab word, Mr. Minkin) as Erica.

I try to ignore her but you can't ignore someone like Erica Dickerson.

Here's the real strike against Erica Dickerson, though.

Today in science lab I have just about enough of Erica so I ask to go to the bathroom. I really don't have to go but I just need to get away from her and I can't stand looking at Chollie with Miranda. I walk around the whole school and after about ten or fifteen minutes I spot Lichtensteiner so I head back to class.

And in class there's Erica with a big smile on her face.

"Hey, this is pretty good," she says, pointing at my notebook.

"What's pretty good?" I say.

"Your book. *Watch This!* It's not bad at all," she says.

Erica has my story notebook.

I'm too shocked to say anything. I mean, who goes looking into other people's things?

"I could help you with that," Erica says.

I just shake my head and don't say a word. It's no use even wasting your breath on someone like her.

Chollie Muller

February 29, 2015

English 8A

Mr. Minkin

Suggested Writing Prompt: *Think about something or someone that annoys or bothers you. Write about what it is and why it bothers you. What can you do to make it less irritating?*

Dear Mr. Minkin,

Sometimes it bothers me when people are mean to each other at school.

And sometimes it bothers me when Coach acts like sports are the most important thing in the world.

And I'm really annoyed that Billy has moved out. I miss him even though it's probably for the best.

And sometimes it annoys me when we do work in groups and no one lets me do anything. It was fun working with Miranda on the Brazilian tapir project, but she did all the work. So I read and wrote about how the gravity of the moon is strong enough to change the direction of the Amazon River. Imagine that. But in the end Miranda didn't think it was important so even though my name was on the report, I really didn't contribute.

And it bothers me that people call me Chollie. My name is *Charles* Muller, but a long, long time ago, way back in kindergarten, I couldn't say Charlie and instead I said Chollie. So now everyone calls me Chollie, even my parents and teachers. But my real name is Charles, with an R, and now I can say Charlie. But it doesn't matter. My name is now Chollie whether I like it or not. And even though it's pretty unfair, there's nothing I can do about it.

Miranda Mullaly
February 29, 2016
English 8A
Mr. Minkin

Suggested Writing Prompt: *Think about
something or someone that annoys or bothers you.
Write about what it is and why it bothers you.
What can you do to make it less irritating?*

Oh, I think I can come up with a few people
that annoy and bother me right now.

Sam Dolan—for hitting my father with a
snowball.

Duke Samagura—for breaking my father's car
window.

Chollie Muller—for ruining the play by not
remembering his line.

Mr. Wexler—for casting Sam, Duke, and
Chollie in the show.

Tom Nelson—for dumping me.

Erica Dickerson—for refusing to forgive me
because of one little lie.

And to keep from wasting paper and my time,

the entire student body of Penn Valley Middle School—for teasing me about what Sam, Duke, and Chollie did and insinuating that I would have anything to do with those three stooges.

Duke Vanderbilt Samagura

29 February 2016

English 8A

Mr. Minkin

Suggested Writing Prompt: *Think about*
something or someone that annoys or bothers you.
Write about what it is and why it bothers you.
What can you do to make it less irritating?

Sir:

My parents, Neal and Cassandra, have been
very annoying. When they found out about the
snow-shoveling disaster (I'm sure you heard
about it, you lover of gossip) they were actually
excited because they thought Sam and Chollie
were my friends and our "fun" got out of hand.
They were so thrilled about me "playing" out in
the snow that they offered to pay Mr. Mullaly the
one hundred dollar deductible for the broken car
window.

Is that really the kind of opinion parents
should have about their one and only beloved
child?

And now they want to host the cast party for closing night of the musical. As the star it is my duty to host it, and I'm certainly happy Neal and Cassandra brought it up. I did not want to be beholden to them.

Unfortunately they insisted on helping me with the invitations. They noticed Sam and Chollie, who are officially listed as cast members, did not get invitations.

"Why aren't you inviting your two friends?" Cassandra asked.

I shuddered at hearing the word friends. "They're hardly in the show," I said. "It wouldn't be right to invite them and not the others cast as Helpers."

Cassandra and Neal shook their heads in disagreement. Because they are sociologists, they become offended and hurt anytime a stranger is offended or hurt. They sensed that Sam and Chollie would be offended and hurt if they weren't invited.

So thanks, Neal and Cassandra, for ruining the cast party before it even begins.

19

Steam Heat

Duke

When I found out Ralph Waldo broke his leg skiing, I thought instantly of Shirley MacLaine.[33] If you've brushed up on your Broadway history, you'll know that Shirley MacLaine became a star after filling in for Carol Haney when she broke her ankle during the original Broadway production of *The Pajama Game*. It was the beginning of her illustrious career. So as I marched to Mr. Wexler's room to discuss replacing Ralph Waldo in "Steam Heat" I thought, of course, of Shirley MacLaine.

But the greatest difficulty of starring in a show with

....

33. The great award-winning American actress and spiritualist.

an incompetent director like Mr. Wexler is the fact that the man lacks imagination.[34]

Here's how it played out:

INT.—MR. WEXLER'S ROOM—DAY

MR. WEXLER sits at his desk, rubbing his temples, running his hands through his hair. DUKE VANDERBILT SAMAGURA stands at attention.

Mr. Wexler

Without Ralph Waldo we can hardly do "Steam Heat."

(Duke looks down at Mr. Wexler, a meager man when compared to Duke.)

Duke

Get ahold of yourself, man! Think. What would Shakespeare do?

(Mr. Wexler is speechless. Duke crosses the desk and pulls Mr. Wexler to his feet.)

....
34. Sherlock Holmes said it was most important for detectives, but it wouldn't hurt for theatrical directors to have imaginations as well.

Duke

Shakespeare would have another actor
substitute for Ralph. I can do it. I will do it.

Mr. Wexler

But the audience will know you as Sid, the
star. It won't work.

Duke

It will. It must.
(*Duke is about to slap some sense into Mr. Wexler
when the door swings open. MISS KERRIGAN
storms into the room.*)

Miss Kerrigan

I've figured it out.
(*Duke and Mr. Wexler turn to Miss Kerrigan.*)

Miss Kerrigan

Chollie Muller. He can fill in for Ralph.

Mr. Wexler

Chollie Muller? He can't even remember
his line.

Miss Kerrigan

I'll teach him. I can do it.

(Duke is visibly disappointed. He releases Mr. Wexler from his grip and walks to the door.)

Mr. Wexler

He is a pretty good athlete. I suppose we have little choice in the matter.

Miss Kerrigan

I can do it!

Mr. Wexler

Let's get to work on it right away.

So now Chollie Muller gets to dance with Miranda Mullaly as yours truly watches from backstage. What a waste of talent.

CHOLLIE

Today in history class Mr. Wexler interrupts and asks to speak with me outside. So I go outside with him and he looks terrible.

"I have bad news, Chollie. Really bad news."

I suddenly get real emotional. My eyes fill with tears and my stomach burns and my heart races and my mouth is so dry I can't talk. I'm thinking something terrible has happened to Mom or Dad or Billy.

"I'm telling you this first, Chollie," Mr. Wexler says, and he puts his arm on my shoulder.

"What happened?" I ask.

"It's Ralph."

"Who?"

"Ralph, Ralph Waldo," Mr. Wexler says.

I have no idea what Mr. Wexler's talking about.

"Ralph broke his leg."

I suddenly let out a big breath. And it's crazy because I didn't even know I was holding one.

"What I'm going to ask you, Chollie, is of utmost importance. Can you handle 'Steam Heat'?"

"I don't know," I say, because I really still don't know what he's talking about.

"I've seen you play basketball, Chollie. I think you can do it."

And then it hits me that "Steam Heat" is a song and dance that Ralph and Sam Dolan do with Miranda Mullaly. I straighten up a bit, as if I've been slouching, and put my shoulders back.

"I can do 'Steam Heat,' Mr. Wexler," I say.

I *have* to. For Miranda.

But it turns out that I can't do it. I really can't do it. Miss Kerrigan tries and tries to teach me the dance steps and I just can't do it. We spend an hour, a full hour, working on the dance steps as I watch Sam sit and talk with Miranda. And after all that time, I still can't do it. Miss Kerrigan finally leaves the stage and Mr. Wexler sends me home, shaking his head in frustration.

I have *all* this going on and I can't even talk to Billy about it.

SAM

So there I am backstage, limbering up and stretching and doing all the stuff you do before you dance a big dance number. And who walks up on the stage with Miss Kerrigan but Chollie Muller.

"Mr. Dolan," Miss Kerrigan says, "Chollie is taking over for Ralph Waldo."

If you haven't heard, Ralph Waldo broke his arm or leg this weekend skydiving or spelunking or doing something else that no one has ever heard of. It was just about the best news of my lifetime because I assumed I'd dance "Steam Heat" with Miranda alone. I give Chollie my tough-guy look, because I want him to know I don't want him dancing with me and Miranda Mullaly.

"Isn't it kind of late to learn it? Maybe it would be better if just Miranda and I do it together."

Miss Kerrigan laughs.

"Why don't you take a seat with Miranda until I get Chollie acclimated to the steps and sequencing."

Miss Kerrigan points to the front row where Miranda is reading a book. I jump off the stage, really excited, since this will give me a chance to talk with Miranda. I can finally bring up *Twilight*.

"Reading a book, eh?" I say to get things going.

Miranda ignores me but that's okay because I know how serious she is about school and books and things like that.

"I really love the Twilight books," I say. "You can bet I'll be in line when the next one comes out."

Miranda looks at me as if I've just farted.

"I loathe, I detest, I despise those books."

I instantly get the impression that Miranda hates *Twilight*. And that's really odd because Erica Dickerson told me once . . . Erica Dickerson! She set me up!

I make a quick mental note to get back at Erica. And then I return my attention to Miranda.

"Yeah, those books are kind of boring. What are you reading there?"

This gets me right back in the game. Miranda closes the book and shows me the cover. It says *84, Charing Cross Road*.

"That looks like a good book. What's it about?"

"It's about a woman in New York City who corresponds with a bookseller in London."

It sounds incredibly boring, sort of like something Sharon would read, but rather than say that, I say, "That sounds really exciting."

Miranda laughs and it's awesome. I mean, what a smile!

"It's not terribly exciting," she says. "In fact, hardly anything happens in the book."

"Then why do you like it?" I ask.

Miranda takes a moment to think about this. I mean, is this a great conversation or what?

"What I like about the book is how these two wonderful people connect without ever meeting one another. But they're connected by their love of literature and history. And their love of books."

Miranda pauses and I think about *Watch This!* and how I can't wait to give her a copy.

"Does that make sense?" Miranda asks.

And just as I'm about to say it makes total sense someone says, "Nothing make sense to Dolan."

It's Erica Dickerson. She climbs over the seat to join us. She even sneaks in between us, ruining the moment like only she can.

20

The Final Dress Rehearsal

Duke

If you know anything about me, by this time you know I do not go for all this newfangled Internet stuff. So instead of sending out impersonal Evites for the cast party, I decided to hand each cast member an invitation. Call me old-fashioned, but I personally think it is the perfect thing to do before the final dress rehearsal. There's nothing like the cast party to put one's mind at ease before the stress of opening night.

It is most important, too, for the star to personally deliver the invitations before the final dress rehearsal. I was most looking forward to handing Miranda her invitation and asking her to join me for ice cream after opening night.

I was a man on a mission as I approached Miranda, stage left. There were lots of cast members all around us, but I didn't care.

"Hello, Miranda," I said.

"Hi, Duke," Miranda replied.

"Here's your invitation to the cast party."

"Thanks," she replied.

She was looking onstage, where Sam was alone, walking through his steps. He looked at us and winked at Miranda. I couldn't believe it. But I wasn't going to let Sam steal my thunder, so I quickly asked Miranda to go out with me.

"I was thinking, Miranda, that perhaps you would like to join me for ice cream after opening night?"

My timing, again, was off. Miranda, I'm fairly certain, did not hear what I said. But Sam Dolan, who rubbed my shoulders in a most mocking manner, asking me if I was ready to go, most certainly did.

Miranda ran off for makeup before I could get a chance to ask her again. Sam was still standing next to me, smiling like an idiot. With all the chaos backstage before the show, it was impossible for me to punch Sam in the jaw, so I walked away, fists clenched.

Then it struck me. The perfect time to get at Sam would be on the stage when I'm supposed to push him in Act 1, Scene 1. From stage left, I watched Sam and Chollie pretend to fix the sewing machines, grimaced as Chollie forgot his one line, then went onstage and rather than push Sam, let him have one square on the jaw. Sam, of course, has no idea how to act onstage and was instantly out of character. He attacked me and I had no choice but to stand up for myself. Mr. Wexler snuck out onstage and broke us up with his clipboard as the music played and the cast danced the next number.

Our dress rehearsal moved along until "Hernando's Hideaway," when Sam attempted to punch me during my dance with Miranda. I will always be a step ahead of dim-witted Sam, saving myself and Miranda from his attacks.

Inexplicably, however, Miranda missed the fact that I had saved her from the hooligan. Instead, she screamed at me when we left the stage, complaining that I was ruining the whole number and the whole show. Then from out of nowhere, Sharon Dolan came up and kicked me in the shin.

To add insult to injury, Mr. Wexler took Sam and me aside and scolded us like an English schoolmaster. I'm sure he would've paddled us if it were legal.

I took a deep breath, rubbed my shin, and planned to get back at Sam one last time. This was far from over.

CHOLLIE

There's this thing that they do in plays called Final Dress Rehearsal. It's when everybody goes through the play one last time before what's called Opening Night. And today is Final Dress Rehearsal.

When I go out onstage to fix the sewing machine, I still can't remember my line, and I freeze up. Mr. Wexler is at the side of the stage whispering to Sam to just keep going. And now it's really official. I don't know what I'm doing and I'm probably going to mess up the whole play. Great, another reason for everyone to make fun of me right now.

But then everything gets really crazy. You see, after I'm supposed to say, "He don't belong in this town," Sid (played by Duke) comes out and pushes Sam's character. Today, though, Duke punches Sam square in the jaw. He really lets him have it. And Sam jumps right up and tackles Duke. No one, absolutely no one, knows what's going on. Then Mr. Wexler runs out to try to break up Duke and Sam.

Since it's the Final Dress Rehearsal, we're told to keep on going as if nothing happened. There's just no time to replace anyone.

What if Sam and Duke fight again? What if I can't remember my line on Opening Night? What if I can't even manage to march in time? What if I run into Mr. Mullaly before or after the play? Maybe I'll save everyone the trouble and not show up.

SAM

I'm so excited for the show that I'm onstage before we even begin the final dress rehearsal. And I have a feeling in my stomach like I've never had before. It's a little bit like telling a joke that gets big laughs, but there's something more to it.

And I haven't had any Mr. Mullaly nightmares for almost two weeks.

I'm in the best mood of my life.

I see Sharon offstage and give her a big wink. And when I walk off the stage, I pass by Miranda and Duke. And when I pass Duke, I put my hands on his shoulders and I say, "Ready to go, big guy?"

Weird, right? But that's just the kind of mood I'm in. I'm even happy to see Duke.

So anyway, we start the show, and I carry the exposition perfectly, if you ask me. Of course Chollie can't remember his line but I'm used to it, so I cover for him. And then Sid, who is really Duke, comes out onstage.

And what do you think Duke, the lunatic, does? He hauls back and punches me in the jaw. Well, I go flying back and then jump up and tackle him. It's the only thing I can think to do. I'm suddenly reminded of how much he gets in my way. The music starts up and Mr. Wexler rushes in to break us up.

He tells us to keep going, but I'm still pretty peeved.

After we do the whole big picnic scene and sing "Once a Year Day," we clear the stage. I follow Miranda and she turns and gives *me* her terrific smile. I mean the kind of smile that makes my knees buckle. The kind of smile she gave me when she returned my thumbtack. The kind of smile I don't see as often anymore.

"You two look great together," Miranda says. And again, she says it right to me.

I stop right in my tracks, and Erica Dickerson bumps into me.

My heart breaks that instant.

Erica smiles and grabs my hand to do our tango. As the music starts up and we begin to dance I suddenly start to feel angry again. I mean, I'm really angry. And when I see Duke doing his tango with Miranda, I get even angrier. I swing Erica toward Duke and Miranda as Erica whispers, "What are you doing, Dolan?"

As I get near Miranda and Duke, I hold on to Erica with my left hand and swing on Duke with my right. But since they're spinning, Miranda is coming directly toward my fist. It's too late to stop, so I close my eyes, getting ready for a huge crash. But my hand doesn't hit anything and Erica and I go spinning across the stage.

I never get a chance to punch Duke, which is pretty unfortunate.

And even more unfortunate is that Mr. Wexler sees the whole thing and starts chewing me out right after I get off the stage.

Even worse is that Sharon won't look at me at dinner and refuses to pass me the ketchup. I don't want to make a big deal, so I have plain meat loaf, which just isn't as good.

I try to apologize after dinner, I really do. But when I go to her room, Sharon refuses to even open the door. And I don't know why, but when I stand outside her room staring at her door, I feel rotten inside.

And now I can't get a good night's sleep because my nightmares starring Mr. Mullaly have returned.

Miranda

To: Erica

From: Miranda

Date: March 15, 2016 9:03 PM

Subject: Cast Party

E,

Can we please, please, please, please, please, please go to the cast party together?

I feel so stupid for even knowing this, but the day of the party would've been my sixth month anniversary with Tom. Are you laughing? Don't worry if you are, I'm pretty pathetic.

And I don't know how you do it with all the energy onstage, but I'm just not feeling it. Are Chollie and Sam really marching behind me? "Steam Heat" is the best part of the play and they ruined it.

Oh well, after today's dress rehearsal I'll be surprised if we even get the show off the ground. I can't wait for this to be over!

OK, last time I'm saying this. Thanks for forgiving me for being such a jerk. You're an awesome friend!

Call me if you want to laugh about the impending disaster.

xoxoxo

M ☺

21

The Pajama Game

Duke

A Confessional

Looking back on it now, perhaps I was temporarily insane. What was I thinking?

I'm covered with a cold sweat as I now begin to realize how rash, how dangerous, how apocalyptic my actions were.

And yet it was all so easy.

I was on a roll, bringing the crowd to its feet with a breathless rendition of "Hey There." And Sharon Dolan really nailed "I'm Not at All in Love." In fact, the entire cast was on fire. Chollie Muller even remembered his line, which is a feat up there with Lindbergh's solo crossing of the Atlantic.[35]

But despite this, I still had in the back of my mind Sam Dolan rubbing my shoulders and Miranda Mullaly walking away from me when I asked her to join me for ice cream. It hurt, and the promise of the musical was not enough to extinguish my burning desire for revenge. I had to do what I had to do, so I went forward with my plan.

I was offstage for a decent part of the second act and snuck around behind the curtains. Armed with an old cane from the prop room, I waited patiently for "Steam Heat" to begin.

Finally the number began, and I lifted up the curtain an inch to see. Miranda and the two idiots began the number, with Miranda leading the way, her talent oozing off of her. Sam and Chollie marched behind as Miranda sang and danced. The audience could not keep their eyes off Miranda, she was that terrific.

For a moment I thought of abandoning my plan. But then from the side of the stage I could see Mr. Mullaly. He looked much more distinguished compared with the last

35. Completed in thirty-three hours and thirty minutes May 20–21, 1927, in the *Spirit of St. Louis.*

time I'd seen him. And best of all, he was even wearing a bow tie. I resolved then and there to show Mr. Mullaly the kind of clown Sam Dolan is.

I waited for Sam and Chollie to march upstage center and then, like an animal awaiting its prey, I quickly snapped out the cane and caught Sam's left ankle, hooking him on my first attempt. Sam instantly lost his balance, stumbling violently forward, but somehow stayed on his feet. A little distraught, Sam managed to get back into the marching routine. I struck again, this time hooking his right ankle and yanking him with all my might. Sam stumbled into Chollie and fell forward, miraculously staying on his feet yet again.

And then I heard it. Laughter. The audience was laughing.

What could be so funny?

I threw the cane under some background paintings and rushed to the side.

There I stood as "Steam Heat" came to an end. The crowd roared its approval, jumping to their feet. Mr. Wexler clapped loudly, screaming, "Bravo! Bravo! Oh, pure genius, Sam. Genius!"

Out in the audience I saw Mr. Mullaly on his feet with the rest of the crowd, cheering for Sam and Chollie.

CHOLLIE

When the show is over, I'm still sort of shocked. I can't believe I didn't make a huge mistake and ruin the whole thing. In fact, I didn't make *any* mistakes. I remembered my line and even Duke Samagura says I "nailed" it, which means something coming from the star of the play.

And best of all is that Billy came home for opening night. I'm so happy to see him after the show. It was all his idea for me to be in the play and it was a great idea.

When we drive home, I'm still pretty excited about the show, and Billy is happy with his new job. It's just about the happiest we've all been since Christmas. Mom is especially happy when Billy says he can stay for only one night.

It's fun having Billy back, and even though it's only been a month, I've missed him. We have a good talk in my room when we get home.

"You really did it, Chollie. Great job."

"I guess I did," I say.

"How's your little friend?"

"Who?" I say, even though I know what he's talking about.

"Miranda. Miranda Mullaly. Any progress?"

"Nope."

Billy's old grin spreads across his face.

"Here's what you gotta do, Chollie," he says.

"It's okay, Billy," I say. And for some reason I lie. "I'm not really into her anymore."

"Okay," Billy says, standing and checking his phone for messages. "I gotta go, but you know where to reach me when you need some advice."

As Billy leaves, I call out to him.

"Thanks, Billy."

"For what?" Billy stops and asks.

"For listening to me and all that," I say. And I really mean it.

"Well, I thought you were terrific up there tonight," Billy says.

I walk over and give him a hug. It's something I've wanted to do for a long time.

"I'm proud of you, kid," Billy says.

Billy tousles my hair and leaves, whistling a tune from the play.

I'm really tired as I hop into bed. And for the first time in a while, I have a smile on my face.

SAM

I'm so nervous about the play I think I'm going crazy.

And the thing is, I'm not worried that I'll mess up or forget my lines or get into another fight with Duke. It's because last night I had another Mr. Mullaly nightmare. Only this time it was when we were doing the play, and this time I wasn't in my underwear but Mr. Mullaly was. And right in the middle of the show, right when I'm dancing "Steam Heat" with Miranda, Mr. Mullaly jumps out of his seat (in his underwear!) and climbs on the stage and starts chasing me. He doesn't catch me, but I feel weak and slow all the same. I don't know what I'm going to do if this keeps up.

So I have all this going on in my mind as we start off with the show. And, don't forget, we had a terrible final dress rehearsal. But despite all this, we did it, we really did it.

I mean, I tripped a couple of times during "Steam Heat" but somehow stayed on my feet. I guess the audience thought it was part of the show because they laughed and clapped like crazy.

Later Ralph Waldo, who watched the whole thing from the sidelines on his crutches, tells me Duke Samagura actually tripped me and that's why I kept falling on the stage.

Can you believe that?

But when the play is over, I don't have time to get back at Duke because now is my chance to see Miranda. Mom gave me a bunch of flowers to give to Sharon after the show. And I take one flower, a pretty red one, and put it aside. This is the flower I'll give to Miranda.

There must be a million people in the lobby after the show and I get the feeling it will be harder to find Miranda than I thought. I see Lichtensteiner in the middle of the crowd, picking his nose. And, of course, Foxxy is with Holly Culver, holding her hand and whispering in her ear.

But then, just like magic, a space opens and I can see her, standing alone at the opposite side of the lobby. And she looks so pretty, with her hair pulled back and a bright happy smile on her face.

I walk steadily toward her and I'm pretty sure something's going to happen. And I'm holding the flower in front of me like it's a great treasure. I can't believe my good luck, I really can't.

But just as I'm about to give Miranda the flower and tell her how terrific she was in the show and how wonderful she is all the time, Mr. Mullaly appears and puts his arm around her like a bodyguard.

Mr. Mullaly is not wearing his underwear like in my nightmares but he *is* wearing a blue suit and a bow tie. The bow tie makes me think of Duke, which just about ruins the whole night. Will I ever catch a break?

22

Serendipity

Sam Dolan

March 21st

English 8A

Mr. Minkin

Writing Prompt: *The dictionary defines* serendipity *as "the faculty of making fortunate discoveries by accident." Write about a serendipitous event in your life. How has the fortunate accident or discovery affected you in a positive way? Explain in detail.*

Hey Mr. Minkin,

You'll never believe it, but serendipity just happened to me this weekend. I don't know if I can explain it but I'll try.

What happens is this. I go to Duke Samagura's

house on Saturday night for the cast party. I'm really excited. I even dust off my thumbtack with the idea of getting Duke to sit on it after what he pulled with the cane during "Steam Heat."

I'm also feeling all right because I saw Mr. Mullaly at the play and he didn't murder me. What a relief.

Duke is real nice to me for some reason when I get to his house, acting like I'm his best friend and all. He even introduces me to his parents, who both look almost exactly like Duke. Totally weird, right? Then Duke brings me along and tells me he's feeling bad about what happened with the cane and he wants to have "a heart to heart" and bury it all in the past. He even has chairs ready for us to have our little powwow.

What's cool is that the chairs are set up in front of a television which is playing the video of the musical. I'm interested in seeing the show, but I don't forget about my little present for Duke. So just as I'm about to sit and put my thumbtack on Duke's seat my sister Sharon stops me from sitting on the chair.

Duke and I don't sit and I have to put the thumbtack back in my pocket. And I'm obviously a little upset with my sister for interrupting my plan but before I have a chance to say anything she and Duke, the two weirdos, start talking about Sherlock Holmes. The last thing I want to talk about is books, so I turn around and there is Erica Dickerson. She sees me and I see her, but it's sort of like I'm seeing her for the first time. I notice her brown eyes and the way her lips curl up when she smiles. And she has cute dimples on her cheeks I've never noticed before.

She smiles and her smile gets me. It makes my skin tingle, and my stomach feels weird, sort of the way it feels when I'm in trouble, but not bad, just different. And I feel really strong, really invincible, like there's nothing I can't do.

So I forget all about dumb Duke and sitting and talking with him. I practically knock people over to get to Erica Dickerson.

"I'm surprised you found the place," Erica says, just like she always says things to me. It's sort of that "you're a dope, Sam Dolan" way she has of talking to me. But for some reason I love it. I love hearing her voice.

I try to say something, anything, to keep her standing there in front of me. But my mind is a blank. I can't think of anything.

"You were very average on stage tonight," Erica says.

Even though I know this is an insult I smile. And I *still* can't think of anything good to say.

"You want me to get you a soda?" I try.

She holds up her hand, and in it is a cup and the cup is filled with soda. I don't want her to leave but my mind is still totally blank. And then, finally, I think of something.

"You were really great tonight."

"Thanks," she says.

"You're welcome."

"Are you okay?"

"I think so," I say.

"Is this all you got, Dolan?"

"No, no," I say. "Um, you know, I'm going to miss practicing—"

"Rehearsing," she corrects me.

"That's right, rehearsing. I'm going to miss rehearsing and all that stuff. It was really fun."

And, boy, do I really mean it. I can't explain how I feel. It's so great standing next to her and talking to her, even if she's only making fun of me and I'm saying stupid things. But at the same time I feel sad, I really do, because the show is over and as it turns out, I liked working with Erica Dickerson.

"Yeah, it was fun, wasn't it," she agrees.

"Erica Dickerson, it was *really* fun."

"We could have one last dance," she suggests. "Or do you think that might be a bad decision that would end up in your book?"

And I am not kidding you when I tell you I took Erica Dickerson in my arms and we danced the tango from "Hernando's Hideaway." I have so much fun I don't ever want to stop. Even when the thumbtack in my pocket gets stuck into my leg and I can feel the blood dripping into my sock, I keep right on going.

And if that's serendipity, Mr. Minkin, then that's my new favorite word.

Duke Samagura

21 March 2016

English 8A

Mr. Minkin

Writing Prompt: *The dictionary defines* serendipity *as "the faculty of making fortunate discoveries by accident." Write about a serendipitous event in your life. How has the fortunate accident or discovery affected you in a positive way? Explain in detail.*

Sir:

It took quite some time, Mr. Minkin, but you've finally come up with a writing prompt worth responding to. I guess even you and broken clocks work once in a while.

Everything worked out just as I had planned after the show. Sam Dolan was one of the last cast members to arrive at my house. I met him at the door, introduced him to Neal and Cassandra, and then personally led him to the rec room where everyone was devouring hot Cheetos, potato chips, and sodas. As Sam descended the stairs there was a round of applause, but we were all in high spirits and full of good cheer, so the applause for Sam did not, surprisingly, give me the urge to push him down the steps.

I brought Sam over to where Neal and Cassandra had set up a loop of digital pictures running on the television. I have to admit after years of bad parenting, they stopped at nothing to make the cast party a success. I pulled out my special chair for Sam to sit on, which I had hidden behind the bar. Just in case, I put a sign that said "Broken" on it so no one would accidentally take it out and ruin my plan.

This chair was special because I had taken out the integral screws that are needed to hold a person. As soon as Sam sat on it, he would crash to the floor.

"Geez, that's pretty cool," Sam said when he saw the loop. Being an idiot, he was instantly mesmerized by the pictures and, of course, being a solipsistic jerk, he couldn't wait for his image to appear.

"There's a great picture of you coming up," I said, pulling up the chair. "Here, take a seat."

"Thanks," Sam said, still watching the screen.

And then, inexplicably, it happened. Sharon Dolan appeared and kept Sam from sitting on the chair and making a fool of himself. And she kept me from getting back at Sam Dolan for the thumbtack and stealing my thunder in the show and foiling the toilet paper plot and ruining the student council. In short, Sharon kept me from getting back at Sam for being the bane of my existence.

I turned to Sharon. I couldn't believe what she had done.

"How did you know about the chair?" I asked, thoroughly appalled.

Sharon pursed her lips in a real cute way, and said, "Unlike most, I see, and I observe."

I was thunderstruck. She was quoting Sherlock Holmes, who, if you've never heard of him, is the most famous detective in the world. I had no idea there was another soul in Penn Valley Middle School so well-read.

I gazed into her eyes. I noticed for the first time that they were blue. Her eyes were kind. And, most importantly, those eyes were interested in me, I'm sure.

I'm certain I've never felt this way before.

How could she be so sophisticated? So talented? So concerned for her fellow human beings? And so beautiful? How could she be all these things and still be related to Sam Dolan, the troglodyte?

"What's the matter?" Sharon asked.

Her voice wakened me from my reverie. I imagined myself in a field of blue flowers, under a grand, shadowy tree with Sharon in my arms.

"I, uh, ah, nothing."

"You looked like you were in a catatonic state," Sharon said, sipping her soda.

Catatonic? Again, I asked myself how this lovely flower could be sprung from the same gene pool that produced Sam Dolan.

"There you go again," Sharon said.

"Please forgive me," I said.

I looked down at the floor for a second, for I didn't want to creep Sharon out by staring continuously into her ocean-colored eyes.

"Might I interest you in a slice of pizza?"

"Sure," Sharon said, smiling at me as I led her away from the stupid chair and from my childhood.

Miranda Mullaly

March 21, 2016

English 8A

Mr. Minkin

Writing Prompt: *The dictionary defines* serendipity *as "the faculty of making fortunate discoveries by accident." Write about a serendipitous event in your life. How has the fortunate accident or discovery affected you in a positive way? Explain in detail.*

I think it was dumb luck, or should I say good luck, that Chollie Muller was my science partner for lab work and the Brazilian tapir research report.

And it was just, I'm sure, simply good luck that Chollie was in the musical and danced, or rather marched, "Steam Heat" with me.

And I suppose that I was really just lucky that Chollie Muller was outside gazing at the stars.

Looking back on it, it's odd I was even outside as the cast party was just beginning. But Erica was dancing with Sam Dolan, doing one last tango now that the play was over. And Sharon

Dolan, who I wanted to congratulate on a great performance, was talking so closely to Duke Samagura, I thought they were kissing. And I suddenly felt very, very alone.

I doubt anyone noticed when I left and stepped out into the backyard. And there was Chollie Muller looking up at the stars. Something drew me to Chollie and I walked across the yard and stood next to him.

"There sure are a lot of stars out tonight," Chollie said.

I nodded.

We were silent for a moment, which was nice. Other boys, especially Tom Nelson, would've started talking about the stars like they really knew about them. Or would ask a stupid question like whether or not there was life out there. But Chollie just said, "There sure are a lot of stars out tonight." It was the perfect thing to say.

I looked up at Chollie and then back up at the stars.

"What do you see up there?" I asked him.

"I see stars and the moon," Chollie answered.

I have to smile to myself because this answer

is so like Chollie. He's always so honest.

"What do the stars and moon make you think of?" I asked.

Again, I looked up at him. For the first time, I really noticed him. And I thought about what it would be like if he put his arm around me.

Finally Chollie looked down from the stars. He looked right into my eyes.

"It's the funniest thing, but it reminds me of a book my mom used to read to me when I was a kid. It's called *Goodnight Moon*."

"That's beautiful, Charlie."

He didn't say anything. But I certainly wanted to hear more.

"It's cold tonight," I said, pretending to shiver.

"You were really terrific tonight, Miranda," he said.

"Thank you, Charlie. And you weren't so bad yourself."

From inside the house we could hear music playing faintly. It was "Once a Year Day" from the show.

"Would you like to dance?" he asked.

I nodded. I couldn't believe how much I wanted to dance with Charlie Muller.

He took me in his arms and led me as if he'd always meant to.

Charlie Muller

March 21, 2016 (Finally got the year right!)

English 8A

Mr. Minkin

Writing Prompt: *The dictionary defines* serendipity *as "the faculty of making fortunate discoveries by accident." Write about a serendipitous event in your life. How has the fortunate accident or discovery affected you in a positive way? Explain in detail.*

Dear Mr. Minkin,

Serendipity is a really nice word, Mr. Minkin. Thank you for teaching it to me.

So serendipity, you say, is like an accident, something good or unexpected happening. But I guess all accidents are unexpected. Otherwise, they wouldn't be accidents.

I don't know if this is serendipity or not. You can be the judge.

I decide to go to Duke's cast party, and I'm surprised he's even invited me since I only had six words to say.

As I'm walking to the party, it suddenly hits me that I'm kind of sad the show is over. It's been fun even with all the trouble I had remembering my line and the dance steps and being nervous and all that.

And I'm still sort of sad because Billy has moved out. Mom said he needed a "little nudge" to get out of the house and both Billy and I know Mom is right. I still hated to see him go, though. It was fun having Billy around, at least in the beginning when he was awake more often.

When I get to the party I suddenly have this urge to punch Duke and Sam in the nose. Not because of Miranda Mullaly, but because they're all having a good time watching the video and fooling around with some chair. And it's a weird feeling because it's not really like me to feel this way, wanting to punch guys in the nose. I'm really confused.

Since I don't want to punch anyone's lights out, and because I kind of feel like crying, I go through the kitchen and out to the backyard. It's a really pleasant night, and even though it's cold, I'm all warm inside. And there are a lot of stars in the sky. Lots and lots of stars. And something about the stars and the moon catches my attention but I really don't know why, if you know what I mean. It's just sort of pretty and quiet and I feel better about being alone.

And then suddenly I notice Miranda Mullaly standing next to me. But for the first time I'm not nervous. I don't know why, but being under those stars makes me think. It makes me think that the world's a really big place and time is kind of going by and we're spinning around the sun and turning and spinning and the stars are so far away we can't ever get to them. And then for some reason I start thinking about this book my mom used to read to me called *Goodnight Moon* and I sort of miss those days. And that makes me think about how the moon's gravity causes the tides of the oceans to rise and fall. I don't know why this stuff pops into my head, but it does, and even though Miranda's standing next to me I keep looking at the stars and not at her.

Finally I say, "There sure are a lot of stars," because I have to say something.

I don't remember what Miranda says next but I can hear her breathing next to me.

She asks me more about the stars, and I tell her how the stars make me think of the book

Goodnight Moon. Saying this makes me feel a little dumb because Miranda reads thick books and *Goodnight Moon* is just a little kid's book.

But Miranda is so great she doesn't even care.

And she doesn't laugh at me.

And then, suddenly, I just say what I feel.

"You know, Miranda, I really liked working with you on the science project and in the lab and I really liked dancing with you even though they made me march."

For a second I want to look up at the stars again because I feel like a fool. But then Miranda smiles at me. She's got a good smile and her eyes are bright and suddenly the stars don't mean that much because I can look into Miranda's eyes. And I don't feel like punching anyone in the nose. And I don't feel like crying. I just feel really, really good inside.

It's kind of quiet and the only sound is music from the show coming from the basement. Then it is all really simple.

"Would you like to dance, Miranda?"

Believe it or not, she says yes and I dance with Miranda Mullaly! Right there under the stars.

And the craziest thing is that for the first time the dance steps come easy.

So I don't know if this is serendipity but it seems like it to me. And I sure can't wait for serendipity to strike again.

Acknowledgments

Special heartfelt thanks to my mother, Nancy Gerhardt, for her unwavering support and faith. And to my sisters, Donna, Maureen, Sharon, and Kristie, and my brother, Timmy. Brothers-in-law Art, V.J., Adam, and Mike along with sister-in-law Kristen. And to my in-laws William Mills Todd III and Eva Andenaes Todd. I am so fortunate to call all of you my family.

I'm indebted to everyone at Viking Children's Books. Special thanks to publisher Ken Wright, Jim Hoover, and Dana Leydig. And a huge thanks to editor Joanna Cardenas for bringing her energy and excitement to this book. Her belief in this book and her editorial expertise have made all the difference in the world.

Dan Lazar, agent extraordinaire, who knew exactly how to get this book into the right hands, and everyone at Writers House, especially Victoria Doherty Munro.

Gratitude to Aleen Keshishian, who made this book happen, and to everyone at Lighthouse Management.

Special thanks to Lulu Troyer for reading an early draft and giving it her considerable stamp of approval. And to Kit Troyer for pointing out the direction I was writing. And Jesse and Boomer!

Thanks to the UCLA Writers' Program, especially Laurel van der Linde, Mary Lynne, Shelia, Glen, and Margaret, and everyone for helping to move this book along with invaluable feedback on late Wednesday nights.

Thanks to everyone at the Society of Children's Book Writers and Illustrators (SCBWI) for creating a network of inspiration and support for writers throughout the world.

Thanks to Pat Walsh, Jay Sefton, and Tom Nelson for friendship and encouragement.

Special thanks to my wife, Karen, and our daughters, Frida and Ada. You make my dreams come true every day.

Mr. Minkin
English 8A
Penn Valley, Room 120

Assignment: *We are fortunate to have the author Jake Gerhardt visiting our classroom tomorrow. Your assignment is a simple one. Write down at least one question you would like to ask him. After his presentation, we will have a question and answer session. Have fun!*

Duke

There's little I find more loathsome than a visit from a "children's" author. In my view, anyone writing books for children can't cut it in the real world of adult fiction and its deeper themes. Oh, well, I guess it's better than listening to you, Mr. Minkin, prove how little you know about the subject you profess to teach.

Here's my question:

I have often heard of, but have never actually experienced, writer's block. What do you do when you have writer's block? Has it ever kept you from finishing a book?

Jake Gerhardt

Writer's block can drive an author mad. Not only do you have the fear that you may not finish your work but you are also overcome with the idea that you are wasting your time. Sometimes when the dreaded writer's block descends upon me I will pick up a book and read. I always make sure, however, not to read a book similar to what I'm writing. If I do, I often feel as if what I'm writing has already been written. Now, that's a rotten feeling, much worse than writer's block.

Character questionnaires are something I use to help me when I feel as if I'm stuck. The questionnaires are filled with questions like, "What's your nickname and how did you get it?" and "What is a secret you have told no one?" or something as simple as "What's your favorite food or movie and why?" When I answer these questions for my characters, I get new ideas about how to continue the story I am writing. I hope this helps.

Chollie

I think it's pretty cool to have a real live author come and visit us. My first choice, though, is to have a professional athlete come to our school. I could ask Carson Wentz about a million questions. Can you imagine what he's feeling as the Eagles' first-round draft pick and future starting quarterback?

Anyway, here's a question I would ask the author:

What's it like when you first show people your stuff? What do you do if people don't like it? Do you ever doubt yourself? What if you write something and it's not very good?

Jake Gerhardt

I am always nervous the first time I share something new that I have written. The first person I show my writing to is my wife, who is super smart and very well read. I can always count on her to be gentle, firm, and honest in her critiques. But no matter what, you cannot have thin skin. You are never going to get it right the first time, no matter what you think. It's simply not the way it works.

In order to keep my sanity, I often think of writing as a sport. Think of your favorite basketball player, and then think of how many big shots he or she has missed. Or think of your favorite baseball player. If he's hitting for a three hundred average, that means he is out seventy percent of the time. Seven out of ten times he fails. It's pretty much the same way I look at writing. Knowing that failure is a part of everything we do keeps me from getting down in the dumps.

Sam

This is perfect, having this author visit us today. First of all, I'm just about out of things to write about for the writing prompts. Come on, Mr. Minkin, you're killing me with all this work. And since I didn't finish my math homework, hopefully I can finish it before this class ends. I'm sure the author won't mind.

Anyway, here's a question for the author:

How did you first get into writing? Did you always want to be a writer? Oh yeah, and usually I find reading kind of boring and never humorous, so how do you write something that is funny?

Jake Gerhardt

I honestly don't think I ever had a eureka moment when I put a book down and said, "I want to be a writer!" I've always enjoyed reading, some books and genres more than others. But it wasn't until I was older and teaching American history and English that I thought I would like to write a book. And because I've always enjoyed writers like P. G. Wodehouse and John Mortimer, I wanted to write something humorous.

Writing something funny is no easier (and perhaps no more difficult) than writing in any other style. But I do know this about writing humor: your readers have got to like your characters and even cheer for them as the story moves along. I think a lot of humor is Sisyphean, meaning that it's about characters who are up against enormous odds to get what they want.

Check out an old Laurel and Hardy short. Ever wonder why they're always moving a piano? Because it's extremely difficult but they won't give up, and it's funny watching them suffer through it. The great comic Mel Brooks once said, "Tragedy is when I cut my finger. Comedy is when you fall into an open sewer and die." So I think the basic setup of three boys chasing after the same girl, though heartbreaking for the boys, is very entertaining for the rest of us. A broken heart, when it's not mine, is actually kind of funny.

Miranda

Thanks, Mr. Minkin, for getting an author to come visit us. I'm fascinated by writers, I really am. And I've never met one before. Even though I love to read, I have never written anything. I get an idea, and then I think about it, and then I start to write, and then nothing. Nothing! It always seems like I have nothing to write about.

Which brings me to my question:

People always say write what you know. But what do we really know at this age? I haven't really experienced anything, so how can I actually write a book? Do you believe that writers should write what they know? Do you write what you know?

Jake Gerhardt

I think that it's true; you have to write what you know,

but only to a certain point. Eventually your characters will take you to unexpected places. And that's the fun of writing: you never know where you're going to end up. (Even if you write a terrific outline—something I don't like to do.)

So my advice is to not ever box yourself in. Use your imagination and take yourself and your characters and your readers to places they never knew existed.

In my writing it helps that I'm in my forties and going on fourteen. I actually really enjoy writing from the perspective of a teenager. It's always fun revisiting my middle school years, both the good times and the bad.

Erica

I find that whenever I try to write stories I always end up telling exactly what has happened in my life. For example, I think it's pretty funny when my dad gets upset with my sisters when they're on their phones. And then I write exactly what he says, but it's never as funny as what I experienced.

Here's my question:

Are there any true things that happened in your life that are in the story? Can you tell us the difference between what really happened and then what happens in the book? How does it get to be different from real life?

Jake Gerhardt

There are many things in the book that started out as something that really happened, or at least was rumored to have happened. When I was about halfway through the first draft, for example, I read about a principal in a school in Pennsylvania who decided to take toilet paper out of the bathroom. Immediately, I thought that was exactly something Mr. Lichtensteiner would do and the result would be hilarious.

The Valentine's Day Dance is really close to what the dances were like when I was in middle school. The gym was split and there really was a continuous basketball game on one side of the gym. Everything about the dances was a combination of excitement and disappointment and embarrassment. The worst thing that could happen, at least in my mind, was when a Duran Duran song played. My female friends would stop dancing with us boys and just dance with each other. It's always, *always* very awkward to walk off a dance floor alone when everyone is having a blast. It feels like every eye in the place is on you. I tried to capture that feeling on the night of the Valentine's Dance.

Mr. Minkin

Thank you so very much for joining us today, Jake Gerhardt. With the time remaining, I'd like to ask a question of my own.

Of all the characters in your book, with whom do you identify the most? Do you share similar traits and characteristics with the main characters and if so, what are they?

Jake Gerhardt

The best part of writing *Me and Miranda Mullaly* was having the opportunity to go back and revisit my middle school years. There's a little bit of me in all the main characters. I can remember feeling the ways Chollie, Duke, and Sam do throughout the book. In fact, there isn't an emotion that they contend with that I did not experience at the age of thirteen as well.

Duke: Like Duke I had an enormous amount of worthless facts in my head in middle school. And like Duke, I often thought if someone (especially one of my sisters) was unaware of a particular fact, he or she was a troglodyte. I would think this even if I'd only learned that same fact the day before. I must've been terrible to live with.

And don't let the fact that Duke proudly wears a bow tie and confidently carries a briefcase fool you. He is just like any other typical teenager: insecure, full of doubt, and often overwhelmed. I certainly felt that way at thirteen. Who doesn't?

Chollie: Chollie is fortunate to have an older brother, even if the advice he gives is always wrong. I didn't have an older brother, but I did have sisters, and on the rare occasions when we were civil to each other (it was usually my fault when we weren't) I always appreciated their help and advice.

What I shared most with Chollie was a love for sports. Football, baseball, basketball, track, just about anything competitive, you could count me in. I definitely needed gym class and time after lunch to burn off my energy. I'm sure my teachers appreciated it when I did.

Sam: If you asked my friends from that time, they would surely say I was most like Sam. I was a bit of a class clown, and the assistant principal had to keep a close eye on me. But I was never in serious trouble, nor was I ever kicked out of class, because I loved being in class. I not only loved watching the teachers teach but I really enjoyed being with my classmates. Probably too much, because I often struck up a conversation with whomever was seated next to me.

Like Sam, I had sisters. I was surrounded by girls, which was not much of an advantage when it came to romance. In fact, when my sisters had their friends over it was really only fun for my friends, who were free to hang out and flirt. My sisters didn't want anything to do with me when I was thirteen. Looking back, I can't blame them.

Although Sam has a plan for his future (to be a stand-up comedian), I had nothing remotely as well planned as Sam. My seventh-grade nephew recently wrote for a school project that he wanted to be a professional athlete or a teacher. That's pretty much how I felt in middle school. What I shared with Sam was the confidence that no obstacle in the future could stand in my way.

I especially enjoyed writing about the relationship between Mr. Lichtensteiner and Sam. I had a similar relationship with the school disciplinarian at my school. He knew I was a pretty good kid, and he personally knew my father and knew that my father ran a tight ship at home. He made sure I behaved, sometimes even made an example of me in front of the other kids. Not fun at the time, but I needed the discipline and attention he provided. Now that I think about it, without his stern hand I may have never learned enough in school to become a writer.

KEEP READING FOR A SAMPLE OF

THE FOLLOW-UP NOVEL

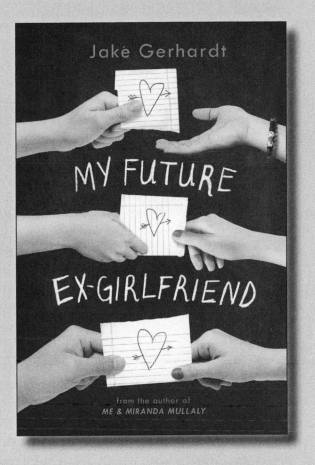

Jake Gerhardt

MY FUTURE

EX-GIRLFRIEND

from the author of
ME & MIRANDA MULLALY

1

All Is Well

SAM

I'M THE FIRST guy at the bus stop, just waiting, waiting, waiting to get to Penn Valley Middle School. Part of me thinks I should just take off and start running, that's how excited I am. But before the adrenaline kicks in, I hear the bus rumbling as it approaches and turns the corner.

Once I'm on and seated, I just feel great, I really do. If we had a flat tire, I swear our bus driver, Ruben, wouldn't even have to jack up the bus. I could just hold it up with one hand while he changed the tire. Are you getting the impression I'm excited for the final stretch of eighth grade to start?

You might be wondering why I'm so eager to get to school. The answer to that question is simple: Erica Dickerson, my new girlfriend. Erica is awesome and pretty. And pretty awesome. We got together just before spring break, and I spent most of my vacation thinking of all the things we'd get to do once we got back to school. Things like:

1. Double-date with my best friend, Foxxy, who hasn't been around as much since he started dating Holly Culver.
2. Sit together on the bus when we go to New York City for our end-of-the-year class trip. Oh, and hang out in the city, I guess.
3. Hang out at lunch together and have a civilized conversation instead of sitting around with the guys making fart sounds and putting butter on the floor to see if anyone slips.
4. Go to the eighth-grade dance! (I won't even mind if my sister's dumb boyfriend drives us.)

I can't wait to tell Foxxy about my plans.

When the bus pulls up to Foxxy's stop, I instantly get the feeling that something's wrong. I can't put my finger on it, it's just that Foxxy doesn't have a grin on his face. And he always grins. As I watch him get on the bus I'm hoping maybe he's just burped up his breakfast or something like that.

"Sam, Sam, Sammy," Foxxy says as he plops down on the seat next to me like it's the end of the day and not the beginning. "You're never going to believe what happened."

"What happened?"

"She did it, Sam. She really did it."

We fall back into our seat as Ruben takes off. He's an awesome bus driver, never in a bad mood. If he has to go to the bathroom, look out, our bus moves like a rocket. Today is one of those days.

"Who did what?" I ask.

"Holly. Holly did it," Foxxy says.

I look at Foxxy. His eyes are red and his nose is running. He looks like he hasn't slept in days. He's a mess.

"What did Holly do?"

"She dumped me, Sam. She dropped me like a bad habit."

Okay, so I don't want to be a jerk, but the first thing I think is that now we won't be able to double-date. And then I remember that Foxxy has a tendency to exaggerate.

"What did she say?" I ask.

"'I never want to see you again . . .'"

"It was probably in the heat of the moment."

"'. . . as long as I live,'" Foxxy says.

"That could be interpreted many different ways," I say, borrowing a line from my English teacher, Mr. Minkin. "Trust me. My sister Maureen breaks up with her idiot boyfriend once a week."

And that's the truth. Maureen's in high school, and she goes out with this knucklehead (and I'm being generous here) named Lutz who's always doing something to make her upset.

"No, you don't understand," Foxxy continues. "She said it to my face. And then she sent me a text. And then I got an e-mail. And then she wrote me a letter, a real letter. And each time, she said she never wanted to see me again."

I look at Foxxy. Snot is dripping over his lips. His skin is pale and looks dry. His hair is uncombed. And his shirt is inside out. Besides that, he looks great.

"How could she honestly say she never wants to see you again?" I ask. "You look terrific. I'm sure she'll fall in love all over again when she takes one look at you."